Under the Willow Tree

And Other Stories

Contents

Diseased

Ripple in the Moonlight

Under the Willow Tree

The Old Writer and the Hungry Squirrels

Our Time Together

The Good Neighbor

Kate's Funeral

Fading Jump Shot

Best for the Family

Secret Lovers

Copyright © 2013 by Jeremy Perry
All rights reserved. No part of this book may be reproduced or transmitted in any form or by electronic or mechanical means, including photocopying, recording or by any information storage and retrieval system, without the written permission of the publisher, except where permitted by law.

Under the Willow Tree

And Other Stories

Jeremy Perry

Diseased

I can't exactly say when I discovered my thinking had become off-kilter. I'd always been a deep thinker, a free thinker, all my life. As a child, I loved sports, the outdoors, and the arts. I had troubles in those formative years, but I never thought I'd feel the repercussions of those misfortunes later as an adult.

Now, I'm old…and crazy, at least that's what the people in the white uniforms have been telling me all these years. They often say, "You're nothing but an old, senile coot, Carter Lynch."

That's why I've been in this hospital forever.

I haven't always been crazy. I do have flashes of happier times in my life, of my family and friends. I remember a time my daughter and I took a bike ride to the park. I remember pushing her in the swing, and she laughed and yelled, "Higher, Daddy, higher!" I also remember proposing to my wife at the lake. She had no idea what I was up to, and I was scared as a little puppy in a thunderstorm.

So, yes, there was a time when I didn't have the *disease*—the term often used in this place. But most of those days I can't remember, only snippets here and there. Lost forever, I suppose. Although, I wish I could remember. I know my memories are in there—somewhere. The people in the white uniforms stopped telling me long ago that I would get better. I guess it's true, but I don't feel crazy.

Tommy Jenkins is another resident who came to Ryker's Ridge Institution a few years ago. I don't know his age. I'm guessing he's half as old as I am. He doesn't say much either. I usually do most of the talking when we have our daily game of Rummy.

This morning he sat across from me eying his cards as if they were about to speak to him, clueing him in on what suit to play next. He looked across the table at me and then back to his cards.

"Will you just play," I said irritably.

He shot back with an annoyed smirk and squinting eyes. I didn't care if I was interrupting his strategy. He had always played in this manner, always taking his time, always dragging the game out at a sloth's pace.

He drew a card from the stack and scrunched his lips to one side, appearing to bite the inside of his jaw. When he did this gesture, I knew he was in deep thought. Finally, he laid a queen on the table.

"See, that wasn't so hard," I said in my most sarcastic tone.

"Bite me," he said.

I scoffed at the remark and said, "Screw you," then drew from the deck.

"Why do you always act like this?"

"Act like what?" I said.

"Like a royal d–bag."

"'A 'd–bag'?"

"Yes, a *d-bag*," he said.

I laughed.

"What's so darn funny?"

"Nothing. Let's play," I said.

Tommy threw his cards on the table. "I'm not playing anymore until you tell me why you're laughing."

"Okay," I said. "You want to know?"

"Yes," he said. He clasped his hands together and laid them on the table in front of him, waiting for my response.

"I was laughing because you said *d-bag*."

"So," he said.

"So. It's funny because every time you try to insult me you can't use the full word. It's always been *a-hole* or *son-of-a-b* or *d-bag*. It really detracts from the insult and makes you look ridiculous."

I watched from across the card table as a mental storm brewed within Tommy. This was the first time I had called him out on his incompetency at verbal warfare. He slid his chair out from the table and bolted upright, scrunching his lips to one side, biting the inside of his jaw.

"Oh yeah," he began. "Well, *f-you*, Carter! I don't need this abuse!" He swatted the stacked deck and cards went flying. He stomped away angrily, across the room and out of my bedroom door.

His outburst made me snicker again. I knew he'd be okay, though. I knew he'd settle down and come to his senses after a bit. I was the only one he had in
this place. I was his only friend. I knew he'd be back. He had always come back.

I can't say exactly for sure how long I've been in here with the people in the white uniforms and the ones who have contracted the disease. Time, for me, has become a mangled, splashing sea of lost memories, ones that I'll probably never recover. But I don't think too much about it anymore, especially today. The people in the white uniforms tell me that today is my birthday. I don't know my age, but I do know I'm old. The man in my shaving mirror tells me this often, as he had done earlier.

"Carter Lynch," he said. "Your face reminds me of a piece of ancient leather. You're old and washed up. On the brink of insanity. In the midst of a slow, agonizing death."

"Maybe," I said. "But I'm not listening to you. You won't corrupt my thinking today. Today is my birthday." I wiped the shaving cream from my face and walked away. He'd always been the negative type, that man in the mirror.

I picked up the cards and restacked them on the table. Not long after, I went venturing out of my room, looking for something to appease my time and warrant myself of a grand birthday. And, like most mornings, I decided quickly on what it was that I wanted to do.

The living room, as it was called on our ward, seemed pleasant today, more than usual. There was a scent of vanilla in the air, telling me the cleaning lady had come and gone. Clarence and Daryl watched another episode of *Bonanza* on the big screen.
Though, I've always thought that they were probably not watching at all—being oblivious to the horses, to the shootouts, to Lorne Greene's deep baritone voice. After breakfast, the people in the white uniforms always led them both there, dropping them off to be forgotten, to soil themselves, eventually.

I walked to the service counter where a tray of doughnuts and bagels and the orange juice machine were sitting. Not everyone on my ward has this privilege, to help himself at the service counter. I've earned that right throughout my years here. Most residents see the orange juice machine and the coffee maker sitting next to it as a threat of some sort, with the sloshing and percolating.

I've seen many residents freeze with fear, or retreat and cry out in agony. I used to do it myself, but time and rational thinking have cured me of that. Although, sometimes when I walk away, I'll look over my shoulder to make sure the machine doesn't decide to follow me. Only to make sure, of course.

I poured a glass of juice and grabbed a bagel from the tray. When I stepped from the service counter, I nearly ran into Pat, the cleaning lady.

"Good morning, Carter," she said. She had her usual rag slung over her right shoulder, ready to do battle with any mess that came her way.

I jumped a little and said, "Good morning, Pat. I see you've been busy this morning. The ward looks very clean."

"Thank you," she said. She stepped around me, grabbed the rag from her shoulder, and wiped the splatter of orange juice and coffee from the counter. I'll admit, every time a mess occurred, whether big or small, Pat would be there on the spot to clean it. I'm certain she had some innate ability to detect clutter and muck. An incredible ability to have, and appropriate for a cleaning lady. "Going out to the duck pond this morning?" she asked.

"Oh, yes," I said. "I wouldn't miss saying hello to my feathered friends. Mrs. Duck should be hatching her ducklings any day now. It's an exciting time."

"Yes. I'm sure it is," she said. "You enjoy your day." And as I began to walk away, she said, "Happy birthday, Carter."

"Thank you," I said with a sincere smile.

I made my way out the front door and into a cool, but sunny morning. Even though today was my birthday, I was unsure of the day or month. Maybe late March or early April.

There was a brisk breeze that slipped through my open robe that made me reconsider coming outside. But I drudged on. I walked down to the duck pond and took a seat on the weathered bench, where I had always come to admire the ducks.

A blinding glare skipped off the water, hitting me in the eyes. I sat my bagel beside me on the bench and blocked the sun's rays with my hand over my brow, looking out and over the pond to find the beautiful ducks. I sipped from my glass of orange juice.

I came out to the duck pond every day to watch the wonderful creatures swim and waddle around in the water. I could tell they loved life and I could tell they loved this beautiful pond. The two of them had come about a month ago when a hint of spring was present, but still too brisk for my old bones to endure sitting outside to appreciate the real enjoyment of their company. I could only watch from the front door of the building, or sometimes I'd catch a glimpse from my bedroom window. They were so beautiful, and I'd realized they were mates when I'd discovered Mrs. Duck sitting on her nest of eggs not long ago. I anticipated the arrival of the baby ducks, and I was certain Mrs. Duck did as well. She was a great mother who tended her nest regularly, never straying far from her babies who, I felt certain, were dying to break free and become full-fledged members of society. I couldn't wait for that day.

Looking around, I couldn't see Mr. and Mrs. Duck anywhere. I sat my juice beside me, tore my bagel into little pieces, and tossed them out into the water, knowing the ducks would come waddling by as they always had.

Out on the concrete path that surrounded the perimeter of the duck pond I spotted an object lying unbothered and unmoving. I gathered my robe at the front and stood from the bench to go investigate.

Walking along the path, I found that the ducks' absence today was odd. I had come out every morning for the last week to admire the little creatures, which would be swimming around without a care in the world. But today was different, and I got a sudden chill the closer I advanced toward the object on the concrete path. A sick feeling, really.

I passed some shrubs and crossed a small wooden bridge, and then, only a few feet away, there was the beautiful little creature. A gusty breeze slipped underneath a wing, causing it to flap and simulate flight. Velvety feathers glistened in the sunlight and were still lovely to behold. However, the duck's small, fragile head had been crushed and a smattering of duck brains and its little crushed bill lie on the ground. A large rock with fresh blood lay nearby. Next to the bank, I saw the nest that mother duck had tended for the last week. Bright yellow goo and smashed eggshells lay in a pile—the remnants of an obvious massacre.

My hands began to tremble and my vision blurred. I was unsure of what to do. The invading panic disrupted my breathing and I felt welling tears forming in my dry eyes. Confused, I wandered down the path, past Mrs. Duck, staggering to the edge of the forest that surrounded the acreage on which Ryker's Ridge Institution sat. I stood there bent over with my hands resting on my knees, crying and gasping for air. My breath was snatched from my body again when to my right, in a ball of blood and feathers, I saw Mr. Duck, looking as mangled and helpless as his female counterpart. I couldn't take any more of this brutality. I ventured down the path and around the duck pond until I was a good distance away from the bloody carnage.

The chilly breeze kicked open my robe, exposing my boxers and white undershirt. But I paid little mind to this uncomfortable coolness. I wiped my tears and after a few seconds of blubbering, I regained my good sense. Was I really crying over these animals? Had my life come to this? This was absurd and unlike me. I'd fought in Vietnam, for Christ's sake. I'd seen enough blood and gore to last a lifetime. I'd seen many a brave soldier with their faces blown off, with mangled limbs hanging from their charred torsos, die in the jungle, in the clutches of my own arms. And now, I was reduced to whimpering like a little school girl, crying because she couldn't find her dolly. Nonsense, really. Pure nonsense. I hadn't cried in years, not since my mother's funeral.

There was only one thing to do. I gathered my composure and went back down the walkway, back to Mrs. Duck and her crushed babies. I had to dispose of her and the nest properly. I couldn't leave her lying there, neglected, at the mercy of the elements or wild scavenging night animals. She and her unborn ducklings needed a proper send off, and I was just the one to give it to them.

Standing over top of Mrs. Duck, I choked back the knot in my throat. Keeping my composure and my manhood intact wasn't as easy as I thought it would be. I began blubbering again. How could anyone treat these harmless creatures with so much cruelty?

I thought about throwing Mrs. Duck over into the edge of the forest with Mr. Duck, but I knew she would be no better off than if I left her lying where she was. Some hungry critter would come in the night and cart them both away. I had to bury them properly. I needed a digging implement of some kind.

Manuel, the grounds-keeper, was already tending to his usual landscaping and yard work. He was walking around with that huge tank on his back spraying the weeds around the building and trees, or anywhere else that a sprouting of unwanted greenery might push through the earth. He'd always called the weeds an *abomination*. In fact, everything to him was an abomination. His low pay, his beat up 1986 Nissan, his little sister becoming pregnant, all of it was an abomination according to Manuel.

With Manuel busy, I knew I could sneak into the storage building and grab a shovel without anyone noticing. The people in the white uniforms didn't watch me with the keen eye as they once did when I had first arrived at Ryker's. I was harmless to them now. Crazy, but harmless.

After getting a shovel, I walked back to the duck pond where the massacre had occurred. I gently lifted Mrs. Duck and placed her on my shovel. I carried her over to the edge of the forest where Mr. Duck lay. I dug a deep hole that both could fit into together, along with their crushed babies. As I was filling in the grave with dirt and leaves, I didn't think about the person responsible for committing this heinous act on these beautiful creatures. I had been blindsided by sorrow. Then, as I recalled the morning events, I began to realize whom it was that had done this. In my mind, there was only one person vicious enough to do such a thing. I returned the shovel to the storage building and went back inside to celebrate my birthday the only way that I knew how.

Everything was much the same when I reentered the living room of the ward. Clarence and Daryl were still watching TV, both in their drug-induced stupors, with their drool and slobber and saturated pajama bottoms. Walking back to my room, I couldn't help but think about the family of ducks that I had buried. I couldn't help but think about the little ducklings that never had a chance to fly, or swim or live. As Manuel would say, this was indeed an abomination.

I sat on the edge of my bed thinking about my dead feathered friends when Tommy stood at my open door, knocking. I invited him in with a casual head motion.

He walked in quietly, with a disposition of a child who knows he's about to receive a harsh scolding. His crime against the Duck family shamefully filled him with guilt. I could see it plainly on his face.

"Hiya, Carter," he said sullenly without making eye contact.

"Come in and sit down," I said, noticing his hesitation at entering my room.

He walked to the card table and sat in his usual chair and I remained on the edge of my bed. "Is there something I can help you with?" I asked, trying to mask my rage.

He sat staring down at his lap, with palms flat on the table.

"I wanted to come by and tell you something." I said nothing. I waited for more. Finally, he looked up and said, "I'm sorry," and then went back to staring at his lap.

Hearing his apology, I waited longer in silence, waiting for an all-out sorrowful confession to the murder of my friends, an all-out testimony to the crime he had committed. I wanted him to say what a horrible, despicable person he was. I wanted him to confess to it all.

I waited longer and the silence prompted him to look up again. When he did, there wasn't an ounce of understanding or remorse upon his murderous face.

Then I said, "Just what is it that you're sorry for?"

He shot me another confused look and I stood from my bed. His lack of sympathy for the ducks made my skin crawl and gave me that uncomfortable, jittery feeling like when I'd had my bad episodes of anxiety attacks many years ago—that being a major reason why I'd come to Ryker's in the first place.

This was my first attack in ages, and I felt it coming on with massive intensity.

"What are you sorry for, Tommy? Just say it, damn it!"

"I'm sorry for calling you a d-bag," he finally said.

"What else?" I demanded. I had to hear him say out loud that he was the one who'd killed the Duck family.

"That's it, Carter," he said. "I'm sorry for calling you that name and cussing you out. I'm truly sorry."

"You killed them," I said plainly and evenly.

"Carter, you've lost your peanuts. I haven't killed anyone." He hesitated. "Are you feeling okay? Should I get the nurse?"

"You killed them. You killed my friends!"

Enraged, I sprang like a lioness going for her kill.

"Good god, Carter. You've lost it!" He tried to escape, but I darted around the card table and blocked his only viable means to a speedy exit.

"I know you killed them," I said again.

I gave him little time to react. I wrapped my hands around his neck and applied a grip that caused his face to redden and his forehead to erupt with protruding bluish-green veins. His mouth spat and sputtered trying to heave a breath of air. He grabbed my arms in an attempt to break my grip. We struggled around the room, beating against the walls, my bookshelves, and then finally tumbling over the card table, upsetting it and the chairs on either side.

My attempt at vengeance was stopped when Dozer, a large orderly wearing one of the white uniforms, busted into my room to separate us. With little effort, he brought me to my feet with one of his tree trunk arms.

"Ms. Montgomery ain't gonna like this," said Dozer with his cross-eyed look and simpleton grin. "You two are in big trouble."

"He's a murderer," I said through gasping breaths.

"I didn't kill anyone," said Tommy. "He's nuttier than a fruit cake!"

I tried lunging at him once more, but there was no getting around Dozer and his super human power.

"You're lying," I said.

"Who's lying?" asked a voice behind me. "What's going on here?"

In walked Ruth Ann Montgomery, the head nurse and manager of our ward.

"Tommy and Carter were having themselves a little go-around, Ms. Montgomery," said Dozer.

"That crazy a-hole tried to kill me," said Tommy.

"You killed the ducks. I know it was you," I said.

"What ducks?" said Tommy. "Ms. Montgomery, I haven't killed anyone."

"He killed them," I said. "Killed them dead. I buried them out on the edge of the forest and—"

"That's enough, Carter," said Ruth Ann. She picked up one of the folding chairs and with her shoe scooted a few of the cards into a pile. "Dozer, get Pat in here to clean this mess. Tommy, go to your room and cool off. Carter, come with me."

I was taken to the holding room where I would wait until evaluated. Many years had passed since I'd last visited the holding room with its padded, white walls and encompassing terror. I had told myself that I would never go back to that hell again. But here I was, deep within the belly of the beast, a place that no one at Ryker's wanted to go.

Sitting in a corner, I was unsure of the passing time. Dozer must have stuck me with a sedative. I was groggy and my anxiety was simmering also. As my nerves calmed, I heard the sliding of the door's lock move from left to right. I remembered that particular sound well.

Walking in was Ruth Ann, with her ever-present casual, confident swagger. Unlike the others who worked at Ryker's, donning the white uniforms, she wore a flowery shirt with a black skirt, which didn't permit the slimming and sleek illusion as the color is generally known to do. Instead, when she walked, her enormous hips rocked side-to-side with each step.

Dozer followed closely behind with a chair and placed it not far from me. Ruth Ann sat, resting comfortably, on the verge of instructing me as to what she intended to do next. I knew the routine. I'd been here before.

I watched Dozer walk back over to the door to stand, as if he were watching over the tomb of the Unknown Soldier. He knew his role. Ruth Ann saw to that.

"So, Carter," she said. "Tell me more about your outburst with Tommy."

I brought my attention from Dozer to Ruth Ann, except, I didn't make eye contact right away. I stared at her swelled ankles and followed up her calves, which were protruding with varicose veins, past her exploding muffin top, and finally looked into her serious eyes.

"I couldn't help it," I said. "Mr. and Mrs. Duck…they're gone."

"Yes, I heard," she said. "But that doesn't give you the right to attack Mr. Jenkins, does it?"

She was using one of her trick questions, and I knew exactly what she wanted me to say. I held my position on the matter. I had to…for Mr. and Mrs. Duck and their unborn babies.

"He's a murderer," I said. "He deserved it."

Ruth Ann crossed her fat legs and said, "Maybe it was an accident. Maybe Mr. Jenkins didn't mean to harm the ducks."

"He assassinated them based on revenge," I said. "Tommy was angered because I had laughed him out of my room this morning. That's all this amounts to—plain and simple."

"I see," said Ruth Ann. She uncrossed her legs and stood from her chair. I noticed her give a nod to Dozer who then walked to where I sat and without effort lifted me to my feet. "Come with me, Carter," said Ruth Ann. "I want to show you something."

I wasn't sure of where I was going, but I was glad I was getting out of the holding room. A person could really go crazy in there.

Walking through the living room, I followed Ruth Ann, and Dozer followed me. When she opened and walked out the front door, I had a good idea of where she was taking me, and I didn't want to go. I tried turning around, but Dozer stopped me, blocking my path.

"I'd rather not go out there," I said in a panic.

"This will only take a few minutes," Ruth Ann said.

I followed her to the duck pond, to the place where the massacre had occurred earlier that morning. My stomach churned, and I felt like vomiting. But I was trapped, no way of turning back, no way of escaping this horrible scene that I was about to relive.

Ruth Ann stopped at the edge of the duck pond.

"Have a seat, Carter," she said, pointing to the weather-beaten bench on which I normally sat.

I eased gently on the bench and turned my head from the water in front of me. I couldn't look, knowing that Mr. and Mrs. Duck would never be there again. I squeezed my eyelids tightly.

"Do you see that?" asked Ruth Ann.

"No. I don't want to," I said, keeping my eyes shut.

"Open your eyes, Carter," she said, sternly.

"No," I said again.

"Do it now or you'll go back to the holding room."

I didn't want to go back to the holding room. I didn't ever want to go back to that awful place. So, I did as Ruth Ann demanded. I slowly opened my eyes.

"What do you see?" she asked.

I hesitated. Out in front of me the water rippled tiny waves in the direction of the bank where Mrs. Duck had kept her nest of unborn ducklings.

She asked me again, "What do you see, Carter?"

And again, I couldn't answer. The wrenching of my intestines worsened and I did indeed vomit, in front of me, beside Ruth Ann. Unfazed, she backed away only a step or two.

I wiped my mouth on the sleeve of my robe and said, "I see the duck pond."

"Look again," she said, grabbing a handful of my hair, tilting my head. "What is it that you see, Carter?"

"The duck – duck pond," I said, looking and shutting my eyes again.

She said, "There is no pond, Carter. There never has been. You need to stop this, this pretending. It's not good for you."

I wasn't pretending. I knew what I saw. I'd come out here to this same bench every morning for the last week with my bagel to feed the ducks, and to enjoy the pristine water and the wonderful morning air.

"I'm not pretending," I said. "Stop saying that. Why are you saying that?"

Ruth Ann bent over a little and spoke directly in my ear.

"Carter?" she said and waited for my response.

"Yes," I said.

"How long have you been a resident at Ryker's?"

I wasn't exactly sure, but I gave the most logical answer.

"A long time."

"Have we always had a duck pond?" she asked, again directly into my ear.

I stalled with my answer. I was unsure. The question prompted me to probe deeper into the archives of my mind, but I still couldn't give an honest answer.

I pinched my eyelids tighter and said, "I – I don't know. I'm not exactly sure."

She said, "I'm going to ask you to open your eyes one more time and then you're going to tell me what you see, okay?" This time I nodded. "Good. Now open your eyes and tell me and Dozer what you see."

I didn't want to, but I also didn't want to return to the holding room. The lids of my eyes slowly parted and I stared out, straight in front of me. In my peripheral view I noticed Ruth Ann motion to Dozer with a pointed finger in the direction of the duck pond. From behind me, the large man walked around the bench.

He walked out into the water, ten feet or so from the bank, and spun to face Ruth Ann and me. Now, I thought *he* was the crazy person, not me.

"Jump up and down," Ruth Ann instructed.

Dozer did as he was told, splashing and rippling the water around him.

"See," said Ruth Ann, "no water."

By now, I was really starting to question her sanity as well.

"But I do see water," I said.

"Look closer, Carter. Concentrate."

Again, Dozer jumped. This time, I saw something, something I hadn't noticed before. The rippling water around Dozer slowly faded. I watched the farthest, tiniest wave and followed it backwards, where instead of getting larger, it slowly erased. And, I no longer heard the splashing sounds.

Agitated, I blinked. I rubbed my eyes until the blurriness went away. I couldn't believe what I was seeing. No longer jumping, instead, keeping perfectly still, Dozer appeared to be standing in a vacant lot or on some sort of cement slab. He was clearly not in the duck pond as he had been only seconds ago. I rubbed my eyes again.

"Do you see it now?" asked Ruth Ann. "Do you see what I'm talking about?" I did see it. But I didn't want to. I nodded. "See, there's no pond or ducks," she said.

I watched Dozer return from the concrete slab.

It was all false, all of it, this entire time. There was no pond. There were no ducks. But what did I bury earlier this morning? Now, I wasn't sure. More make-believe moments from a time which I had thought had been real. But Ruth Ann Montgomery convinced me otherwise. Was it a pile of leaves? Trash? I became frightened by this detachment from reality. I'd rather I hadn't been told.

"Come on," said Ruth Ann. "It's over. Let's go back inside."

I walked away from what once was a pond that had not only reflected the beautiful sky on its placid water, but had also released a culminating brilliance of love and life upon my battered being and relieved a little unspoken heartache and misery each day that I had to spend at Ryker's Ridge Institution.

The three of us went back inside the building, which I had always tried to escape, and I attempted to enjoy the rest of my birthday. Going straight to my room, however, I laid down to rest. I wanted to forget about this exhausting day.

When I awoke the next morning, I felt invigorated. I had slept wonderfully and had all but forgotten the happenings of the previous day. Today, I felt alive and very well.

I dressed myself and walked out to the living room where Clarence and Daryl watched television, intently, unblinking, and never moving. I smelled the air and again I knew Pat had already made her rounds of cleaning the ward. I walked over to the service counter to pour myself a glass of orange juice and grabbed a bagel from the tray.

Walking outside, I noticed a bright sun hovering above the eastern horizon, and the morning dew glinted off the green grass. The day was beautiful already.

I made my way to the weathered bench and sat my orange juice beside me. Looking out, the pond was more magical than ever. I saw the beauty in it as I always had. I didn't care what Ruth Ann Montgomery had to say. I loved this pond, and I was going to keep it.

I tore my bagel in half, and from that, I ripped tiny pieces, throwing them out and into the water. Not long after, from around the bushes, over in the farthest corner of the pond, swam Mr. and Mrs. Duck, followed by a trail of little ducklings.

"Well," I said to the family of ducks, "I see congratulations are in order."

The family of ducks swam to the floating pieces of bagel and helped themselves. When the first half of bagel was consumed, I tore the other into tiny, bite-sized morsels and tossed them out to my feathered friends.

I enjoyed the ducks' company and they enjoyed mine. And that's all that mattered to me.

~~~

Ripple in the Moonlight

Watching another classic showdown on the last day of school was the perfect ending to another boring year. I stood back and cheered for my pal Michael Conway. Michael was small, but he knew how to scrap. In fact, I had seen him in many fights, and he had won almost every one.

Michael's opponent, Jerry Sullivan, was a bully and a bruiser who stood nearly six feet and weighed at least 180lbs —and the kid was only in the sixth grade, same as Michael and me. I was pretty sure he had failed a grade or two, although I couldn't prove it because he had moved here in the third grade.

The brawl seemed to go in quick, exploding bursts. And up until this point, the fight had been nothing more than fat mother insults and ugly girlfriend remarks, followed by another round of wildly thrown punches and rolling around on the grass.

"Well, your girlfriend is a bitch and the ugliest thing that walked the face of the earth," said Michael.

"Oh yeah," Jerry began. "At least my mom can take care of me and I don't have to live with my grandma."

It was at that moment the vibe of the cheering crowd took an abrupt change and fell silent. Knowing Michael since the first grade, I knew his mom had struggled with substance abuse and that he'd been forced to live with his grandparents. He hated talking about it, and to him, it was a painful subject. But now, everyone standing there knew about it. I was sure something horrible was about to happen. That's when all eyes fell on Michael.

Michael stood there with his fists balled at his sides, more serious than ever.

"What did you just say, you son-of-a-bitch?" he asked Jerry.

"You heard me. Your mom is a druggie and everybody knows it."

You could sense the fear in Jerry's tone as he repeated the statement. Michael stood motionless and glared with a grave expression that spoke volumes. It was then Jerry realized that he had chosen the wrong insults.

Michael thundered toward Jerry in a blind rage. The crowd went back to cheering and shouting as he unleashed a quick, right jab to Jerry's mouth. He followed with a forceful kick to the groin, which produced a guttural moan from the bigger boy. Michael then wrestled Jerry to the ground, yelling.

"Don't you ever…I mean ever…talk that way about my mom again!" He straddled Jerry with his hands around his neck. "I should kill you right now!"

I really thought he was going to choke Jerry to death. Luckily, the angels were looking down on him that day.

"Hey, man, get up," I said, tugging at Michael's shoulder. "Ms. Jones is coming. Come on, get up. She's gonna see you!"

The recess teacher was indeed on her way to investigate the stirring commotion. Without hesitating, Michael removed his death grip and sprang to his feet.

We darted across the recess yard trying to make our getaway as discreetly as possible. Once we got to the tire swings, I knew we were in the clear.

Swiping away the grass and dirt from his clothes, Michael said, "I really messed him up, didn't I, Andy?"

"Hell yeah you did!" I said, still feeling the rush of adrenaline from watching the fight. "You tackled his big butt on the ground. He was scared to death."

"I can't believe he said that right in front of everybody, though." Michael knocked away the last few pieces of grass from his left shoulder. I could see the hurt in his eyes, so I tried to comfort my pal.

"Don't worry about what that butt munch says. He doesn't know you. He was only trying to make you mad."

"He knows me now," Michael said, grinning.

I returned the smile and said, "Ain't no doubt, buddy. After that ass whipping, he'll remember you for a long time."

"Hey," said Michael with a jolt. "We're still going camping tonight, right?" And just like that, our twelve-year-old minds moved on to priorities that were much more important. The fight had temporarily dismissed the thought of our camping trip from our memories.

"Hell yeah, we are," I said. "I've got all my stuff packed and ready to go. My dad said he'd drop us off."

"Cool," said Michael. "Is Danny still going?"

"I haven't seen him any today. But I talked to him last night on the phone and he said he was."

"Awesome," said Michael. "Won't be nothing like it. All alone out in the woods—camping and fishing."

"I know. I can't wait either," I said.

So we made it through the rest of the school day without any more distractions, and thankfully, Michael wasn't caught for fighting. If he had been, I'm sure his grandma would've changed her mind about letting him go camping. And that would've been a terrible start to our summer vacation.

Just as he had promised, my dad dropped off Michael and me at Myers Lake around six o'clock. There was no one else there which meant we'd have the entire lake to ourselves. Once we selected our campsite, we immediately began assembling my old canvas tent. After that, Michael dug a pit for the campfire, and I rigged our rods and reels for cat fishing. Next to the bank, we dragged an old picnic table, which would give us a place to sit while we fished. Later, we both gathered firewood and in no time our outdoor adventure was starting to take shape.

After organizing our camp, it was time to get down to some serious fishing. I took a seat on the picnic table and Michael joined me. We sat quietly, lost in thought, only speaking to each other here and there. I don't know about Michael, but I felt like a real man of the wilderness. Here I was, surviving by my God-given ability to live off the land. I looked around and the sun was shining, the birds were singing, but more importantly for us, school was out. We would have all summer to do what we wanted. It was a great feeling.

"Are you sure Danny is coming?" asked Michael as he cast out.

"That's what he told me," I said, concentrating on the tip of my pole.

"Maybe he's not—"

"What's up, gentlemen!" yelled a voice. We whipped our heads toward the dirt road that ran alongside our campsite. Beyond the row of pine trees, I could see someone walking in our direction.

"Danny!" we yelled back.

Danny Shuler was a seventh grader who went to the same school as Michael and me. He walked in with a duffel bag slung over his shoulder, a fishing pole in one hand, and his Coleman lantern in the other. His bright, red hair was glowing as usual.

"I see you guys started without me," he said.

"Only been here about an hour," Michael said.

"Yeah, you haven't missed anything. They're not biting at the moment," I said.

Danny placed his camping gear on the ground and said, "Well, gentlemen, never fear because I've brought alternative means of entertainment. In my bag are a few items that every young man I know will enjoy."

Michael and I placed our fishing poles on the ground and went over to investigate.

"What the hell you got in there, a naked woman?" Michael asked, grinning.

"As a matter of fact..." And then, Danny revealed from his bag a copy of *Playboy* magazine.

"How did you get that?" I asked, trying to grab the little treasure from his hand.

"I swiped it from my dad's collection," he said, yanking the magazine from my reach. "He won't even know it's missing. But that's for later." He placed the magazine back in his bag, rummaged once more, and pulled out a bundle of bottle rockets along with a brick of Black Cats. My fantasies of naked women, for the moment, had exited altogether. Lighting explosives was at the top of every young man's *must do* list.

"You think we'll be able to make some noise with these babies?" asked Danny.

"Hell yeah," said Michael. "I'm always game for blowing up stuff."

"What else you got in there, Shuler?" I asked. "Come on. Give up the goods." I tried looking into the bag, but Danny closed it before I could catch a glimpse.

"Be patient, my young friend," he said. "Lastly, what I'm about to show you has put grown men on their asses. It has pushed young, fledgling greenhorns, *like you*, into manhood." He reached into the duffle. "Gentlemen, I now give you...*white lightning.*"

"That's what I'm talking about!" wailed Michael.

"Well, I say we keep fishing," I said. I turned back around to regain my spot at the picnic table. I wasn't much of a drinker so the booze didn't excite me much.

"Gentlemen, gentlemen," Danny began. "I assume you haven't ventured very far from your campsite?"

"What the hell are you talking about?" asked Michael.

"On down the path is a swinging rope. You know...that suspends out over the lake," explained Danny.

This was definitely more my style. "Let's go check it out," I said.

"Come on. I'll show you," said Danny.

"Hey, bring that bottle. I might want a little sip of that," said Michael.

After reeling in the fishing poles, we made our way down the trail. We walked maybe a hundred yards from camp, and there it was, just as Danny had said. Tied onto a huge maple tree, the rope extended out and over the water. I knew we were destined to have some fun now.

"I think somebody put it up last summer," said Danny. "It should be pretty safe."

"Looks safe enough to me," I said. "I'm going for it."

I didn't hesitate. I stripped down to my boxers, scooted down the dirt embankment, and waded out to retrieve the rope. The lake mud squished between my toes, and the water was not warm at all. But I had committed and there was no turning back now.

"How's the water feel?" asked Michael as I climbed back up the bank.

"Nice and warm," I said.

Michael said, "Yeah right, asshole. I know better than that. I dare you to do a flip."

"You have any last requests?" asked Danny while pretending to hold an imaginary microphone in my face. I stretched the rope back and worked up my last nerve. "Yeah, don't drink all the liquor." I then bolted for the water.

I jumped out and over the lake until my swing was at its highest, released, and landed in perfect cannonball formation. When I resurfaced, a round of cheers greeted me.

"That wasn't a flip, you ass munch," said Michael.

"Your turn, Shuler," I said, clambering back up the slippery embankment.

"Maybe later," said Danny.

"You mean I'm the only one that's getting in?"

"I'm starting to get the urge to take a little swig from this bottle," said Danny.

"It's cool, Andy," Michael chimed in. "We'll all go off the rope later. Let's have a few drinks and maybe set off some bottle rockets. Maybe catch some fish?"

"All right," I said. "But you're both going in later."

"Sure," said Danny. "We'll both go off the rope later." Michael nodded in agreement.

"Okay. Well, give me a drink then," I said.

Like I said, I wasn't much of a drinker, as I'd drunk alcohol only one other time before. That incident had me heaving chunks of my mom's meatloaf into my cousin's bathtub. It had been a bad experience. Nevertheless, I reached for the bottle and started to take a sip, but before it reached my mouth, I noticed my pals had already helped themselves to a quick snort or two. The bottle was no longer full, and I turned to them with a surprised look.

"You guys are assholes," I said as they both burst into laughter.

I went ahead, took my drink, and proceeded to hack and choke.

This junk is awful, I thought.

I continued to cough and moan until finally I caught my breath. "Damn, that's good stuff," I strained my voice to lie.

Danny laughed and gave me a slap on the back. "Come on," he said.

As he and Michael started back up the trail, I too started to see the humor. I picked up my clothes and followed my pals. Actually, the moonshine wasn't half-bad. I actually liked it.

Returning to the campsite, Michael said, "Hey, guys, I'm going to light this fire."

That sounded like a great idea to me. I was feeling chilled from my short swim and was ready to warm up. The sun was nearly down and the temperature was dropping. Danny also ignited his lantern and set it on the picnic table closer to the water, giving us better vision of our rod tips in the dark. We baited our hooks with fresh chicken liver and set line to water. We sat on the ground, three in a row, and watched the stars pop out in the darkening sky.

Moments after casting out, Michael said, "Say, pass me that bottle."

"You sure you want it?" asked Danny. "You're not going to get all choked up and carry on like our good friend *here*, are you?" He gave a nod in my direction. "I don't need both of you acting like amateurs."

I didn't care that he made fun of me. I wasn't a big drinker and I knew my limit.

"Just pass me the bottle and I'll show you *amateur*," said Michael.

"Let's all take a drink," I said.

"That's a wonderful idea," said Danny. "You can go first, Mr. Conway." Danny shoved the bottle in Michael's direction.

"Ok, *Daniel*, don't mind if I do." Michael grabbed the bottle with authority and unscrewed the cap. He then turned the contents straight up and chugged three enormous gulps.

Holy cow! I thought.

He screwed the cap back on the bottle without missing a beat and handed it back to Danny. "Your turn," he said while wiping his mouth.

Danny wasn't to be out-done. He grabbed the pint bottle, looked over at me, and gave a sinister smile and then a wink. He unscrewed the cap and began to drink as if he had been doing it all his life. Michael and I watched as the redheaded wonder gulped down four colossal slugs. After a slight cough, he handed me the bottle.

I looked nervously at each of my friends. Michael was already on his way to Buzzville. He looked on with glossy eyes and a smile that seemed to be a permanent fixture across his freckled face. Danny was more composed. He sat in anticipation, as I too would momentarily join the higher ranks. I reluctantly pulled the bottle up to my lips and let one huge swallow roll down my throat and into my belly. The fiery liquid set my internal organs ablaze, but I didn't commence to spitting and choking as before.

"Hell yeah," said Michael. "Now that's how ya drink, boys. You'll get…the hang o' it…sooner or later, pal," he said to me as his words slurred and his head swayed back and forth.

"Not bad, Andrew," said Danny. "Not bad at all. We'll make a drinker out of you yet." He gave me another slap on the back.

"Hey," I said abruptly. "Why don we shoo off them fire crackers?" My tongue seemed to quit working properly and my head began to spin.

"Yeeahh," Michael agreed, although his body didn't. When he tried to stand, he planted both feet firmly on the bank, but quickly fell over, face down in the dirt, laughing. "Maybe I jus stay here fo a bit," he said.

Danny and I laughed.

"Damn, he's messed up," said Danny.

"Aah, he'll be ok. Prolly jus needs to sleep it off. Les shoo sum fire crackers," I slurred again.

"Sure. Okay," said Danny.

Danny handed me a full pack of Black Cats from his duffle bag, and without warning, I threw the unwrapped explosives into the fire. We both took a few steps back and waited. As the wax paper burned through, the firecrackers exploded into a frenzy of deafening pops and cracks. The noise did not faze Michael. He continued to rest peacefully on the ground in his deep, drunken sleep.

Danny opened the package of bottle rockets and placed four in a row across the picnic table. He pulled a lighter from his pocket and lit them one-by-one. The pint-sized missiles took off with a piercing shrill and followed up with a loud pop. We continued until most of the firecrackers were gone and boredom began to invade our adolescent minds. However, I soon rediscovered the *Playboy* magazine in Danny's half-open bag. The night still showed promise.

I sat by the warm fire scanning the glossy pages. My young mind had only dreamed of naked beauties before, but now, they were right in front of me. I continued to gaze down at the pages in amazement. I hardly noticed Danny grabbing the lantern off the table and heading down the path. The fishing poles didn't exist anymore. My intoxicated pal, lying on the ground, went undetected as well. I was looking at some *real* women, unlike the undeveloped girls in my class. These women were great.

A little while later, my concentration was broken when I heard a thud of a splash. And then I heard Danny yell, "Come on, Andy. Get your butt down here. The water feels great!"

Yeah right, I thought. *You ain't fooling me. I know how that water feels.*

"Yeah...Ok. I'll be down there in a second." *That should hold him for a bit.* I was more interested in looking at the naked girls in the magazine than freezing my butt off again. "You go ahead, buddy," I mumbled.

Danny continued his flying acrobats from the rope. Before and after each swing, there was a chant of celebration, a spout of recognition, letting the world know he was king of the rope.

"Are you coming or not?" he yelled down the bank once again. "I'm not going to stay young forever. Get your ass down here, Andrew!"

"I'm coming, you ass munch." I finally gave in. I stood up and staggered down the shadowy path, cussing under my breath. I didn't want to get back into the icy water; one time was enough.

As I approached the maple tree, I heard Danny once again blare out his trademark yell before splashing into the water.

"Man, I'm only jumping, like, one time," I said as I took off my shoes. My stirring anger was somewhat sobering. "You hear me, asshole?"

I faced the water and repeated myself. I could see the water rippling in the moonlight. "I'm talking to you." Suddenly, I got a stroke of fear. "Danny, come on, man. This isn't the time to be messing with me. Where you at?"

I began to panic so I eased down the bank and into the water. "Answer me, damn it. Don't screw with me, asshole!" I swam out into the dark water, screaming. There was no answer. I dove down into the murk hoping to discover my pal. The lake was too deep and my strength was fading. I swam back to the shore and made my way up the bank, panting fiercely. I yelled out again to Danny. Then, I ran down the path and back to camp in an attempt to wake Michael, but he was out cold. I ran back to the rope and went in once more. Again, I was at the mercy of the deep, murky water.

My endurance no longer existed and my mind was in a disarray of fierce panic and confusion. I wasn't sure of what to do so I swam to shore. Every second felt like an hour wasted. I threw on my pants and shoes and went running down the dirt path, past the campsite, and out to the main road. I ran to the nearest house for help. I wasn't giving up on my friend.

Not long after, the local sheriff's department arrived and I had to explain what had taken place. Then, after about an hour of searching, the dive and rescue team finally pulled Danny's body from the chilling depths of Myers Lake. When we saw our friend's lifeless body emerge from the seemingly calm water, Michael and I were heart broken.

As I looked on from a distance, I tried to understand the tragedy that I was witnessing. I came to realize that I had lost a good friend, one that I could never get back.

For some strange, unexplainable reason, between the chaos and confusion, I began wondering if maybe, just maybe, there was a rope in Heaven, and someday Danny and I could take that swing together.

I could only hope so.

~~~

Under the Willow Tree

Our house sat five hundred feet off the busy highway. I built that house myself and knew exactly how far from the road it was. Beige vinyl siding covered the outside and a lengthy porch lined with patio furniture and a wooden swing stretched across the front. If I had to size it up, it was a modest looking house, for sure.

Scattered throughout the ten acres on which the house sat were many trees. There were pine trees, maple trees, oak trees, and even a green apple tree in the back yard—but my favorite was the weeping willow. I had planted the willow about fifteen feet adjacent to the curve in the sidewalk, just outside our kitchen window. That was ten years ago, soon after I had finished building that house and we had moved in.

Despite the house's inviting outside appearance, it had endured hellish activity on the inside. Fighting and arguing was common between my wife and me. We often disagreed on many

issues, petty arguments, really, as most generally are. I remembered a time we'd argued over who the better weatherman was—channel three's meteorologist or channel seven's. Another time she screamed at me, calling me an idiot for mowing the grass the wrong way. She insisted I mow in the direction that blew the grass outward instead of inward.

"Sure, dear," I had said.

"Do I have to tell you how to do everything?"

"Of course not, dear," I replied.

"Then get your head out of your ass and do something right for a change!"

"Yes, dear, of course," I said.

My friends always questioned my sanity and wondered how I could possibly live with such a 'tyrant,' as they often called her.

"She's not that bad," I had said in her defense.

"Sorry, Gene, better you than me, ol' pal," they would say.

Even with the fighting and belittling, somewhere buried deep within me was a strong, unexplainable love for my wife. A love that would often come seeping up out of the smoldering rubble that was our marriage, telling me everything would eventually be okay.

Today, like most days, we were in the middle of yet another one of our famous spats.

"Where are you going?" I said, standing in the doorway of our bedroom.

Anna shoved shirts, shorts, bras, panties, and other clothes into her suitcase.

"I can't stay here," she said. "I can't do this anymore." She was on the verge of tears.

"Do what?" I asked. "Be married?"

"Yes, you idiot. Why do you think I'm packing?"

I sipped from my glass of bourbon and then said, "But I thought we were happy?"

She stopped long enough to glare in my direction. "No, Gene. *You* thought we were happy. Why couldn't you see *this* isn't working? Why couldn't you change?"

I took another drink from my glass and thought about the question for a moment. I said, "If you weren't happy, why didn't you tell me?"

Anna slammed the suitcase shut, zipped it, rushed passed me and out the bedroom.

At least once or maybe twice a month she would try to leave. I knew she wouldn't, really. She was waiting for me to stop her, waiting for me to beg her to stay.

I followed her through the living room and into the kitchen where she finally stopped at the back door. Standing there, she looked so delicate and fragile. She appeared helpless, like a lost little girl, with her blonde hair gathered into a short ponytail. She turned to me. Her chin dropped to her chest and tears began flowing down her roundish, fair cheeks. I set my glass of bourbon on the deep freezer and walked over to where she stood.

"Don't cry," I said. "We can make this work." I wrapped my arms around her.

She set the suitcase on the floor and then buried her face into my chest and cried. After collecting her feelings, she stared up into my eyes.

"This is so hard," she said. "I pray to God every night to give us a baby. I only ask for one." Again, she cried and buried her face into my chest.

We'd been trying to conceive for the last five years. Each negative result plagued Anna with deep depression. Some days she would lie in bed all day. I tried reaching out to her, but her sorrow would never allow her to listen to me.

"I have no doubt you'd be the best mother ever," I said. "You know, we can still consider adopting. Maybe we should call Pam down at the adoption agency and set up another appointment?"

She pulled away from me, wiping her eyes. Her sad outlook on the world vanished, replaced with a volatile stare.

"Why? Do you think I can't have a baby? Maybe it's *you*, Gene. Maybe you're the one who's to blame."

I smiled and took the abuse, like always. "I can call her first thing tomorrow morning?"

Anna said, "Well, maybe you should. Besides, what do I have to lose?" She sighed deeply and walked away, leaving me and her suitcase alone by the backdoor. She walked into the kitchen, found a bottle of wine in the fridge, and poured herself a glass. I reclaimed my glass from atop the freezer, and went out the backdoor to sit in the hammock beneath the willow tree.

The next morning, which was Saturday, I called the adoption agency and our caseworker, Pam, was able to get Anna and me in for an appointment that afternoon.

When we walked into the small office, I noticed everything was much the same as when we had visited Pam two years prior. A towering, oak bookcase stood in the corner lined with various editions on parenting and spiritual guidance. A picture of Pam and her family sat on the window ledge behind her office chair. Children's coloring pages graced the front and sides of her desk. The office was pleasant and welcoming.

Other than a lingering hangover, I felt great, and I was optimistic about our meeting. Anna seemed happy as well. When I had gotten off the phone with Pam that morning, Anna's aura had changed from gloom to a beam of hope. I was glad she was happy and not wanting to fight with me. It was a nice change, for sure.

"It's great to see you again," said Pam, sinking into her chair.

"Thanks for seeing us on such short notice," said Anna.

"Yes, thank you," I said.

"Not a problem," said Pam. "I had a husband and wife cancel this morning so everything worked out perfectly."

I tried to hold Anna's hand, but she flicked mine away, which didn't surprise me.

Pam pulled our file and we told her we were still looking to adopt a baby girl, and this time we were going to see the process the entire way through. Our previous attempt hadn't survived because we couldn't agree on the baby's name.

"You want to name the baby after your mom?" Anna had said, with disgust in her voice. "The poor kid will be picked on for the rest of its life with the name Henrietta."

"Henrietta for the middle name," I had suggested calmly.

"I won't have my child going around with a goofy name like that." And, of course, the discussion, along with our adoption journey, ended there.

After a series of questions and a review of our old case, Pam said, "Well, everything looks in order. Do you have any questions before you go?"

Anna said, "So how long do you think this whole thing will take?"

"I can start the initial process by this evening," said Pam. "I'll do a data base search and see if we can find a potential match for you and Gene. Sometimes matches come up quickly and other times it could be months." She paused and leaned forward. "The most important part about your adoption journey is to stay positive and continue to support each other." I got the feeling that Pam was seeing right through us.

Again, I reached over to grab Anna's hand and, this time, she took mine. I couldn't believe it. She even smiled a little. Things seemed to be heading in the right direction. Even the drive home was pleasant. We talked to one another the entire way, laughing and joking and feeling optimistic about the adoption process.

Later that evening, we chose to celebrate by inviting Anna's parents over for dinner and drinks. We couldn't wait to tell Blake and Sue of our great news.

After dinner, we all gathered in the living room. Blake sat in my recliner, and Sue swayed back and forth in the rocking chair beside her husband. Anna and I sat on the sofa, across from her parents.

Sue was a large, wholesome woman. Sitting in the rocking chair, her hips pressed through the side spindles of the armrests. Anna's dad was a short, broad-shouldered man who slouched no matter what he was doing.

Anna and her mom sipped from glasses of red wine while Blake and I drank highballs. On her third glass of wine, Anna sprang the news. I couldn't wait for Blake and Sue's reaction. I knew they would be happy. With no other grandchildren, they had been cheering for us to conceive for a long while now.

"That's nice, dear," said Sue. Without further reaction, she broke into a conversation about how Anna needed flowers for the front porch. "Looks drab," she said. She twisted her thick neck toward her husband. "Blake, don't you think it looks drab?" With his slouching shoulders, he shrugged mildly in agreement.

I knew things were about to get heated. I watched as Anna leaned up and scooted to the edge of the sofa. "Didn't you hear what I said? I'm going to adopt a baby."

I couldn't let that slide. I broke in to correct her.

"Actually, *we're* going to adopt a baby."

Sue held out her empty glass. "Gene, dear, get me some more wine."

Anna drank the rest of her wine and said, "I'll have another, too. And fill it to the top this time."

Saying nothing, I took Anna's stemmed glass, walked over and smiled while Sue handed me hers.

"Fill mine up, too," she said, without a please or thank you.

While in the kitchen, I fumbled in the side door of the refrigerator and tried to listen in on the conversation. Half-empty bottles of wines, champagnes, and liqueurs were in a jumbled mess. I grabbed the soft red from the door and, as ordered, I poured the glasses to the brink of spilling over. Still in earshot, the conversation continued.

"Did you hear what I said?" asked Anna.

Sue answered, "Of course, dear. But didn't you try this once before? Why don't you and Gene keep trying the natural way?"

By this time, I had re-entered the living room with both wine glasses brimming to the top.

Anna said, "It's because Gene here," she gave a nod in my direction, "can't produce the goods. His swimmers are lame, apparently."

Here we go. I always got the blame.

"We don't know that for sure," I said in my defense. "I've never been tested. In fact, neither of us has been tested."

"My eggs are just fine," said Anna.

"How do you know?" I asked, handing the full glass of wine to Sue.

"And how do you know they're not?" Sue said to me.

I looked over to Blake, seeking some sort of male support. Instead, I received a confused look and a reluctant shrug.

"Well, I don't know for sure," I said.

"That's right, you don't," said Sue. I watched her take a sip from her glass and, unknowingly, she spilled blots of red wine across her white blouse. I took my place on the sofa, secretly happy that her white blouse was now most likely ruined.

Normally, I wouldn't waste a single breath arguing with insensible people, but after four highballs, I was feeling game. Besides, this was my house. I didn't have to listen to this ridicule. I got enough of that from my wife practically on a daily basis.

I asked Sue, "What makes you such an expert in fertility?"

She huffed. "You don't have to be an expert or a doctor to figure out where the problem lies. It obviously comes from your side of the family."

On the coffee table in front of me sat the bottle of bourbon from which Blake and I had been drinking. Next to the bottle, sat my mini cooler filled with ice. I opened the lid, scooped a handful of cubes, and dropped them into my glass. Unscrewing the cap from the bottle, I said to Sue, "I wasn't aware you knew my family lineage so well. Please, tell me more about it."

Irritably, she huffed again. She twisted uncomfortably in her seat and the wooden rocking chair creaked loudly. What a sight it would be if the flimsy chair gave way and Sue went crashing to the
floor, spilling the rest of her wine all over her particularly small bosom. It didn't happen, but was a gratifying thought, nonetheless.

"Well," Sue began. "You were an only child, and if I do recall, your mother had you later in life. The result of some type of fertility issue, I'm sure. Wasn't she thirty-eight or something?"

"Thirty-three," I said, and drank from my glass. "Not an age I would consider too old to have children."

By now, Sue's face glowed. It felt great knowing I was getting under her skin. I was giving the old bitty a taste of her own medicine. But I knew the moment was too good to last. It never did.

"Gene, this conversation has nothing to do with us adopting a baby," said Anna. "Why are you trying to start an argument?"

"Me? She's the one who accused—"

"Just be quiet," said Anna.

I wanted to defend myself, but if I did, I knew I wouldn't have a fighting chance. Competing with the stubbornness of my wife was more than I could sometimes handle. Adding her overbearing mother to the mix only caused my input on certain matters, including this one, to become less important than it already was—nonexistent you might say.

Instead of lashing back, I rose from the sofa without saying a word. I walked into the kitchen and looked out the window.

The sun set just off the horizon and the western sky was shades of mauves and pinks and greys and blues. In the foreground was the weeping willow, encompassed by the array of spectacular colors. For me, this image brought inner tranquility. I had been to art shows, county fairs, and museums, and there I had seen paintings that tried to capture this enthralling time of the day. As talented as the artists were who created these pieces, none could match the magnificent brush stroke of Mother Nature.

Interrupting my thoughts were two loud, drunken hyenas laughing in the living room. Anna and her mom went from badgering me to belittling Blake. I have to say, he did make for an easy target. Like the other times, his short stature invited the brunt of his ridicule.

A hair-raising cackle from Sue sent a cold shiver down my back. She said, "And I still have to buy all his clothes in the boys' section of J.C. Pennys!" She barely got out the last word when both mother and daughter burst into laughter. Sue's high-pitched shrill made me cringe yet again. I sipped my bourbon, threw my attention back to the beautiful sunset, and tried to forget about this horrible evening.

The next morning, the blaring ring of the telephone awoke me. When my eyelids peeled open, the sunlight shooting through the window hit me in the face, and I flinched and glanced away.

"Would you please answer that?" I asked with my backside to Anna. It rang again and I said, "Honey, will you please get the phone?"

The phone continued to ring and I got no response from my wife. I rolled over and found she wasn't beside me. So I scooted across our king-sized bed to stop the annoying ringing.

"Hello," I said.

"Hello. Gene? Is this Gene?" asked the person on the other end.

Through a deep yawn I said, "Yes, this is Gene."

"Hi, Gene, this is Pam from the adoption agency. How are you?"

"Oh, hello, Pam. I'm fine."

"That's great," she said. "I'm calling to inform you and Anna that we may have found a match for you—a six-month-old baby girl from Russia."

I swung my legs over the side of the bed and stood quickly.

"That's wonderful," I said. "Let me find Anna. Hold on just a minute, Pam."

"Sure. No problem," she said.

I held the phone to my chest, scrambled out the bedroom door, and yelled out to Anna.

"Anna? Pam is on the phone. She has great news!"

I couldn't wait to tell her. I entered the living room, but all was silent except for the humming of the central air unit. Then, I realized today was Sunday morning, the time Anna usually takes care of the laundry. I walked into the kitchen, approached the laundry room, and still heard nothing. I brought the phone back to my ear.

"Pam, are you still there?"

"Yes, I'm here."

"I'll have to call you back. Thank you, though. I know Anna is going to be very excited."

"You're quite welcome," said Pam. "Just call back in the next day or so to schedule an appointment."

"Okay. Thanks again."

"You're welcome."

"Bye," I said.

"Bye–bye," said Pam.

I set the phone down on the kitchen counter and watched out the window. Beyond my willow tree, I noticed Anna's car at the end of the driveway, and after a line of cars passed, she eased out onto the busy road. She hadn't mentioned that she was going out this morning, but that wasn't uncommon. Normally, Anna came and went as she pleased.

I went back to the kitchen counter where the phone lay to call Anna. At the far end, I saw a sheet of paper.

My first thought was Anna had actually left me a note to tell me where she was going. I picked up the note to read it.

Gene,

You were an asshole last night. I'm sick and tired of all this fighting. I can't do this anymore. And please don't try to stop me this time. If you need to talk just call my cell. I'll be staying at Mom and Dad's until I find a place.

Anna

I placed the phone and note back on the kitchen counter. Out the window, I studied my weeping willow tree. I watched as the morning sun shined brightly down on this glorious gift from Mother Nature. The tree was a spectacular sight to marvel. It had grown rapidly throughout the years. Its branches hung low, but not too low—just low

enough to lie in my hammock beneath them, comfortably shaded. It made me happy to see it doing so well. This tree was something I had appreciated for the longest time. Then, deep within me, I developed an even bigger appreciation for this tree. It occurred to me that my willow tree and I were alike in many ways. More so than I had ever thought before.

In the passing ten years, the willow had endured on going abuse from the unpredictable elements. Harsh winters brought freezing ice and heavy snows, which caused the branches to bend, sometimes cracking and breaking. The tree had also seen its share of parching droughts, ones that baked its radiant green leaves to a burnt crisp. Somehow, though, this wonderful tree persevered through the backlash of Mother Nature's trying moments, and, much like the willow, I knew I too would overcome life's backlashes. I knew I too would persevere with resilience.

After eating a bowl of cereal, I dressed and before stepping out the backdoor, I grabbed Anna's note off the counter, wadded it up, and tossed it into the garbage can. Stepping around the outside corner of the garage, I inhaled a breath of fresh air and the sunshine struck my face. I smiled as I felt the invigorating warmth of the sun's rays. I walked over and underneath the willow tree I settled into my hammock. I stretched my legs and admired my sprawling ten acres. I thought about my wife leaving me, and at that moment, I felt more alive and freer than ever before, just like my weeping willow tree.

~~~

The Old Writer and the Hungry Squirrels

It was an ongoing chatter of squawks and barks that rattled Ian McAllister from his sleep. This noise woke him the same time every morning, but there was no one to blame for it except Ian. Two weeks earlier, he had nailed an empty soup can onto the outside ledge of the kitchen window and filled it with handfuls of corn. Two lively squirrels had accustomed themselves to this routine and were awaiting their daily handout.

The old man opened his eyes and looked high above to the square, wooden ceiling beams running parallel with his bed. They ran from one wall to the other, adding to the sound structure of the one room cabin.

Slowly, he swung his legs over the side of his bed and slid his bare, boney feet into his house slippers. He yawned, stretched, and stood, joints stiff and cracking.

"I'm coming, you rascals," he said, scratching his round belly from over his nightshirt.

He grabbed his walking cane that was beside his bed and paced wearily to the kitchen cupboard. He opened the door and scooped a cupful of corn from a small burlap sack. When Ian raised the window, the squirrels leaped to the snow-covered ground and returned to the ledge after he filled the can and shut the window.

"There you go," said Ian, looking on as if he were a proud papa.

With pleasure, the old man watched the squirrels—the large red one, which he had named Arthur, and the smaller grey, dubbed Maxwell—nibble yellow kernels between their tiny paws, standing on the window's ledge.

What fascinating creatures, Ian thought, standing in front of the frosty glass. Lifting his gaze, he looked past the furry squirrels beyond the grey fencing that surrounded his front yard, and out to the wooded hillside. Ian marveled at the pine trees blanketed with fresh fallen snow. He loved this secluded countryside that he had called home for more than thirty years. He reveled in the wonderment of the morning, and shortly after, stepped away from the window and sidled over to the coffee pot.

It had always been these little things—the playful squirrels, the beautiful landscape—that had brought comfort and joy into Ian's life. Such were the small pleasantries of a lonely writer, whose wife had died long ago, and who was without anyone to call a friend.

After making his coffee and pouring himself a cup, Ian ventured a few steps over to his roll-top desk. He set his cup on top, eased down in a cushiony chair, and leaned his cane against the side of the desk. The desk had been his grandmother's and the smell of her stale pipe tobacco still permeated the old wood, which hurled him back to his youth every time he sat down to write.

The old writer pulled out his notebook, and with pen in hand, he stared down to yet another intimidating blank page. He contemplated a plot line that he had been mulling over, but found it weak and disposed of the idea.

"That'll never work," he said. This was his common response to any inkling of creativity that he had had in recent months. It was the mindset that had ruled his thinking much of the passing year.

Creating stories had become a struggle for Ian. He had run into nothing but disappointing dead ends. However, he had never given up. This life, the one of a writer and storyteller, was all he knew. Every day he drudged forward, hoping to revamp his creative talent which he fervently believed was lying somewhere within.

He grabbed his coffee cup, sipped, and again glanced over to the kitchen window—adjacent to his desk—to watch the squirrels devour the kernels of corn. The squirrels were the only reliable entity in Ian's life. They brought him comfort and happiness.

Again, Ian sipped and then placed his cup on top of his desk. He returned his concentration to the vacant page of his notebook and tapped his pen mindlessly, searching for the slightest glimpse of hope.

"If only I had a muse that I could count on," he said while twisting the end of his white mustache.

Several minutes passed and still no words or ideas came forth. He rotated his neck, trying to unbind the stiffness which was setting in faster than usual. An hour went by and then another and not a single scribbling of a sentence or word occurred.

Becoming frustrated, Ian slumped in his chair and said, "Damn you, muse! Where are you? I need you more than ever."

With his fingertips, he massaged his head at the temples and again he glanced to the kitchen window and noticed the squirrels were gone. They had gotten their free meal and headed back to the wooded hillside.

In a small way, Ian felt used. Maybe it was loneliness causing his feeling of dismay. Maybe it was his inability to create the marvelous stories for which he was once widely known. Whichever the case, he had never felt this way about the little woodland squirrels.

"You creatures are like all the rest," he said. "You're no different from the agents and publishers who are constantly putting their grubby hands into my pockets."

As Ian finished his complaining and looked again to his notebook, a discharge of knocks came from the front door of his cabin. He was not one who startled easily, but he jumped slightly and expelled a few obscenities under his breath. He grumbled and rose from his chair.

More knocks came and Ian grabbed his cane and walked across the one-room cabin. When he turned the deadbolt and opened the door, the old writer's eyes gazed upon a being that made his bitter heart flutter and dance.

"Good afternoon, Ian," said the visitor.

Ian stared giddily. Standing before him was the most beautiful sight he had ever seen—a woman with hair as black as the night sky and complexion equal to that of the fallen snow behind her. She wore a long, elegant red dress that sparkled in the sun's reflection. Draped over her shoulders was a shawl fashioned from the fur of an exotic animal.

"It's you," he said. "What are you doing here?"

She walked through the doorway, going past him.

"My goodness," said the woman, "someone could catch a deathly cold out there." She rubbed her arms, as if trying to induce circulation back into her limbs. Ian shut the door behind her, and his enchantment of her soon turned to irritation.

He asked, "Why are you here, Tamara?"

The elegant woman unfastened her shawl, exposing vast cleavage and ample breasts. Ian took notice of her sexual allure. It had been years since he had witnessed such erotic splendor. From the tips of her shiny high heels to her long, straight locks, he absorbed it all with much delight.

"My, aren't we getting touchy in our old age?" said Tamara. "Can't a person stop by and see a dear friend whenever she wishes?"

Ian said, "I'd never realized we were such *dear* friends." He turned his eyes from her enormous bosom and headed back to his desk.

"Surely you don't mean that," said Tamara. We've been friends for so many years. Don't be so bitter, Ian."

He said, "How am I supposed to feel? You've been away for a long time now."

"Yes, I know I've neglected you," she said with a voice absorbed in guilt. "But I'm here now, aren't I?"

Ian ignored her out of spite. He grabbed his pen and thought he might write a line or two. For a moment, he had truly felt a jolt of inspiration. And at last, he did write. He jotted two brilliant sentences.

He had loved her dearly. The pain and agony grew within him each passing day.

Ian stopped writing, sat back in his chair, and stared down to the page.

"I haven't been able to do that in months," he said, astonished.

Tamara said, "It feels wonderful, doesn't it, Ian— to produce your prose once again." While she spoke she stood behind him, watching over his shoulder.

"Yes, it does. I've been waiting for this moment a long time."

"I know you have," said Tamara. "I heard your wish. That's why I've returned to you. As you said, you *need* me. And there are plenty of wonderful stories floating around inside that magnificent mind of yours, waiting to make you a best seller once again. I can make that happen, Ian, just like before."

Ian turned in his chair and with suspicious eyes stared up at her.

"How can I be sure you won't leave me again? How can I be certain that I can trust a muse like you?"

"Muses do come and go, Ian. We all know that."

"True," said Ian. "But I don't care for that uncertainty. I've lived this way for far too long. I need to know that you'll always be there when I need you. And I'm old. I don't have much time left."

Tamara leaned over, pressing her large breasts on the back of Ian's neck. She breathed heavily and seductively into the old writer's ear. Ian's old heart thumped in his chest.

"Now, Ian," she softy whispered, "we've been through this all before. We both know what it will take so that you're able to write your stories at will. Better yet, so that we'll be together forever. Doesn't that sound wonderful? Nothing has changed, Ian. My offer still stands."

The feel of bare cleavage on his neck and the smell of Tamara's exotic perfume sent a pleasing chill down Ian's back.

"But why must I sign over my soul?" he asked, remembering the terms that she had introduced the year before. "There must be another way."

The seductress sank her hands into Ian's shoulders and neck and intricately massaged his old, tired muscles.

And again she lowered herself, whispering into his other ear.

"I wish there were, Ian, but I'm afraid there isn't. The gods of the underworld will need your immortal soul if you wish to write as you did before. That is the only way. You owe it to your fans."

For the old writer it seemed like ages since he had published any respectable works. It had also been ages since he had received his last piece of fan mail. Ian missed that connection with his readers, the corresponding back and forth. He missed touching their lives as he had done when he was a young, prolific writer. He wanted to be the free-spirited writer from the days of old.

"And you can promise me the words will flow as freely as I please? No more struggling. No more misery?"

"Of course," said Tamara. "I promise all that—for the rest of your days."

Ian pulled away from the muse's persistent pawing, grabbed his cane, and pushed up from his chair.

"I'm still not convinced," he said, walking over to peer out the kitchen window. He hoped to catch another glimpse of his furry friends, and he wished he had not felt so bitter toward them earlier.

"How can you say that?" asked Tamara. "Wasn't that wonderful feeling of writing a few moments ago convincing enough? Ian, you can have all that again and so much more. All you have to do is give up your soul. Hand it over and write as you've never written before."

Staring out the window to the snowy hillside, Ian listened to the words of his muse. She continued her swooning and coercing. The longer she talked, the more sense she made. He was tired of this burden of being unable to write, but most of all he was heartbroken because he was unable to enjoy his craft.

Ian turned to Tamara. "Okay, I'm ready." After a moment of silence and a deep breath, he said, "Take my soul and do with it as you wish. I don't need it. Just give me back my will to write."

Tamara walked over to Ian, her high heels clacking on the hardwood floor. Smiling, she placed her soft, pale hands on either side of the writer's whiskered face and caressed gently.

"You've made a wise decision, Ian," she said in a caring tone. "Your love of writing will return as will an outpouring of story ideas that will indeed touch your fans, just as you have wished."

She pulled her hand away from his face and darted toward the front door.

"Wait. Where are you going?" asked Ian. "I thought we were going to be together forever."

Stopping at the front door, Tamara refastened her shawl and turned to him.

"I'll always be with you in spirit, Ian. And I'll drop in on you from time to time. When you awake tomorrow morning, everything you've wished for will be as it should be."

Tamara walked out the front door leaving a skeptical old man in her wake. Ian did not attempt to write any more that evening. Instead, he would wait until morning to see if the muse stayed true to her word.

After a night of unsettled sleep, Ian rose again to the squawking sound of the squirrels. He was glad to see they had returned.

"Here you are," said Ian, dumping the corn in the soup can.

This time he did not admire the critters while they ate. Instead, he brewed his coffee and quickly took his seat at his desk to continue with the wonderful story he had started the day before. Relaxed and confident, he pulled out his notebook and pen.

With little effort the words and ideas streamed from Ian's pen onto the page. He could not contain the huge grin emerging on his creased face.

"Remarkable," he said to himself, energized as he continued to write.

After only an hour, Ian had completed an entire story. And it was not just any story; it was one of brilliance. He felt as if it were one of his best. Reading over the finished work, he basked in the joy and comfort of something he had not been able to do for a long time. Most importantly, he felt no different. He did not feel like a man who had lost his soul. He was not even certain that he had. He was however convinced of one thing: he could write again. To Ian, this was all that mattered.

Day after day, until a week had passed, Ian repeated his routine of feeding the squirrels, preparing his coffee, and writing his stories. Each story, saturated with the old writer's style and flair, possessed a quality unlike any story of the present day. To Ian, each one appeared almost lifelike. And in true Ian McAllister fashion, each story covered his favorite subjects: chaos, death, and destruction. He had written many stories of this nature throughout the years, but none as magnificent as the ones he had churned out in the past days.

One evening while in the midst of another writing session, Ian stopped briefly to read over his work. This story was starting out to be even better than the one he had written the day before. He thought this could possibly be the greatest work to date.

His starry eyes scanned the page and again he noticed the intricacies of his writing, possessing realism unlike anything he had ever written before. It had been so long since he felt this way about his craft and he sensed his talent as a writer was improving day after day. The old writer fed from this natural high and felt Tamara had indeed held true to her word; although, he still did not feel like a soulless scribe.

While Ian wrote, Tamara, all charm and allure, again appeared at the front door wearing the same dress and shawl that she had worn on her original visit.

"I've noticed you've been a very busy man, Ian McAllister," she said, walking into the cabin, high heels clacking on the hardwood floor.

"Oh yes. More than ever. You're truly remarkable, Tamara. I won't doubt you again. Thank you for all that you've done for me."

The muse walked over to Ian's desk and gently ran her hand along its top and down the side.

"I've come to thank you as well, Ian," she said, admiring the craftsmanship of the wooden desk.

Perplexed, Ian said, "For what? I've done nothing—nothing that I know of."

She picked up Ian's notebook that lay on his desk.

"Your stories are changing the world, Ian—even as we speak. The gods of the underworld are extremely pleased with you." She quickly flipped through the pages of stories.

"Please forgive me," Ian began, "but I haven't submitted anything to my publisher. My fans, or the rest of the world, know nothing of my stories."

Tamara threw the notebook back on the desk and laughed.

"You really have been busy, haven't you," she said. "Even too busy to know what's going on all around you."

"What do you mean?" asked Ian.

"Turn on your television."

"My television? Is this some sort of joke?"

"It's not a joke. Just turn on the TV," Tamara said again.

The old writer shuffled over to the end table by the sofa and picked up the remote to the television. Hesitantly, he aimed and pushed the power button.

When the screen's illumination was at its fullest, Ian saw flashes of brutal chaos and destruction. This was something often showed by the news stations so it was nothing unusual for Ian. He glanced over to Tamara.

"What is it I'm supposed to be witnessing?" he asked.

"Flip to the next channel," said Tamara, watching the screen, intently, enjoying the scenes as each played out one by one.

Ian did as she said, and again the screen displayed the same bloody suffrage.

Breaking News, the headline stated. *Many Dead after Today's Catastrophic Earthquake.*

Somewhat rattled, Ian flipped to the next channel.

"Bodies burnt alive," said the news anchor. Again, the old man changed the channel.

Every station depicted mayhem—nothing but widespread death and chaos. The old writer became uneasy and sensed something was not right, in fact, something was eerily wrong. He turned off the television and tossed the remote onto the sofa.

"What the hell is going on?" he asked.

"You've gotten your wish," said Tamara, elated. "Your words have once again made a huge impact on the people of the world."

It was then Ian understood her. All the turmoil on the television mirrored that of the stories in his notebook—the topics Ian loved to write about most: pandemonium and destruction.

"You mean I'm responsible for all of this?" He gave a nod to the television.

"I'm afraid so," said Tamara.

Ian stood stone-faced; not wanting to believe the moment was real.

"You fooled me," he said through a trembling voice.

"Nonsense," said Tamara. "I've made you the most prolific writer in the world—just as you wished for. There was no trickery involved."

"You are evil in the purest form," said Ian. "How could you have allowed this to happen? Innocent people are dying!"

Tamara said nothing. Instead she walked over to a painting hanging on the cabin wall.

"For an old man you are naïve," she said. She bumped the frame a little to the left, squaring it with the other pictures hanging on the wall. She turned back around. "Evil is everywhere in the world, Ian. Don't you see that? It's greedy people like you who spread evil. If you hadn't bargained your soul for your precious writing career, none of the destruction would be happening right now. You're the only one who's to blame. Not me."

Ian was not sure how to respond. He thought for a moment, and then stood up a little straighter and blurted out the first logical thought that came to his mind.

"Then I'll quit writing."

Tamara laughed. "I'm afraid it's not that simple. You've made a deal with the gods of the underworld. They will force you to write your stories. And even if you try to stop, you won't succeed. You are without a soul, Ian. You have no choice in the matter."

Ian was in disbelief. He had always been a gentle, caring man. He had never wished any harm on anyone. He had always loved Mother Nature and the woodland creatures, and he respected his fellow man. He had no idea that one day his words would lead to worldly devastation.

Walking to the front door to leave, Tamara said, "I hope you understand this has nothing to do with you personally. Good and evil have always existed in the world, Ian, and it's always been a balancing act between the two. I hope you understand. And I want to thank you for your contribution." She walked out, shutting the door behind her. The old writer dropped his cane and quickly walked over to turn the deadbolt.

Distraught, Ian nervously ran his fingers through his white hair. He walked to the kitchen cupboard, pulled from it a bottle of whiskey and a glass, and unscrewed the lid from the bottle. With his shaking hand, he poured a generous shot into his glass and gulped it. He poured another and drank again. Ian tried not to think of his stories but was unable to avoid them.

With every attempt to sway his mind, Ian found himself steering back to his latest story. Ian grabbed the bottle of whiskey and his glass and made his way back over to his writing station. After sitting, he poured another, this time filling the glass to the top. He took a large gulp and then placed his glass where his coffee cup normally sat. He opened his notebook and with pen in hand he began to write.

Even with concentrated effort, Ian was unable to stop himself from writing and so he eventually gave up and let the muse's influence prevail. Subconsciously, he was aware that the story was of pure evil, although he did not mind. It was the writing, the act of creating, the act of producing art, something that he had missed for far too long, that took over his being. He had always loved and valued the art form, and did so as he scribbled out the words in his notebook. But at the same time he loathed it as he never had before.

On and on, into the early hours of the morning, he wrote with nothing holding him back.

Finally, Ian stopped and looked down to his words when a welling tear broke from his eyelid, rolled down his whiskered cheek, and splashed onto the page of his notebook. He wrote one final sentence, scooted from his desk, and made his way to the bedroom area of the cabin.

It was an hour later when the sun started rising above the wooded hillside, just past the grey fencing that surrounded Ian's front yard, that the frolicking squirrels were already at the window's ledge, wanting their morning ration of corn. For a solid half hour they squawked, barked, and played, trying to capture the attention of the one who had been feeding them regularly for the last couple of weeks. Even with the squirrels' playful persistence, the one who filled the soup can did not come to the window this time.

Through the frosty window, past the old, roll-top desk, a shadowy figure gently swayed from one of the square, wooden ceiling beams of the log cabin. Ian McAllister's lifeless body hung suspended by a stretched rope that had elongated his neck to unnatural proportions. No more would he hurt anyone else. No more would this caring man have to worry about wreaking havoc on the world with his words. Ian McAllister had written his last story.

On the desk with the half-filled bottle of whiskey and empty glass, sat Ian's notebook, and on the bottom of the last page of his final story was his final request:

God, forgive me.
And someone please feed my squirrels.
Ian McAllister

~~~

Our Time Together

Jimmy had a difficult time keeping still. He squirmed and grew restless in his chair and waited as patiently as any nine-year-old boy could wait. He attempted to watch his favorite television program in order to send his thinking in a different direction. But there was no use. The growing excitement the boy felt on that late summer evening exceeded beyond anything that he had ever experienced before. He was on the brink of receiving the most glorious of gifts, one that meant everything to him, one that would make his dreams come true.

Jimmy Harrison was an undersized kid. He wore a pair of cut off denim shorts and went shirtless, just as he had done all summer long. Sprinkled with dark freckles was his tiny nose. Most of his tangled hair hung well over his ears, while the rest tried desperately to escape the confines of his worn out Little League cap. Turning in his father's reclining chair, he looked nervously out the window behind him.

"When is Dad gonna be home?" he asked his mother. "He should've been here like an hour ago."

"Just relax, honey," said Sandra Harrison. "He hasn't been off work for very long. He'll be home soon enough."

Jimmy's mom was a petite, soft-spoken woman who did not have a lax bone in her tiny body. In her waking moments, there were always chores that needed doing.

"See...look. I told you," she exclaimed as she unfolded the ironing board. "He's pulling in the—"

Before she finished, Jimmy bounced out of the reclining chair, sprinted out the front door, and jumped off the porch. He bolted through the yard and leaped over his bicycle just to greet his old man.

Allan Harrison rolled into the driveway just as he had done every evening after working a ten-hour shift. His spirits were high and his favorite country-western station blared from the speakers of his 1985 Jeep Laredo.

With the Jeep still rolling down the driveway, the eager lad ran alongside, demanding answers. "Did you get it? Did you get it?" asked Jimmy, shouting over the music.

"What? I can't hear you, Jimmy boy," said Allan, teasing. He kept the radio's volume at its max. "What in the world are you talking about?" he yelled back, bearing a juvenile grin, the cigarette hanging from his mouth staying securely in place.

"Oh, you know *what*," Jimmy hammered back while nervously pumping the bill of his Little League cap. "Did you get my shotgun?"

"Oh...is that all you wanted?" asked Allan. Finally stopping, he turned off the Jeep, rolled-up the windows, and got out.

Jimmy's dad was an average-sized man who stood around 5 feet 10 inches and weighed nearly 200 pounds. His once prominently flat stomach from his twenties no longer existed. Now, at the age of 35, his mid-section stretched the buttons on his navy-blue work uniform. He had a mustache that was dark and thick and hid his upper lip from the rest of the world, giving him the appearance of a western outlaw from long ago. Smudged proudly across his face was the day's work from the forging plant, just as it was every day at this time.

"Well, Jimmy boy..." he said and paused with a brief sigh. "I did stop to look at the Remington you'd picked out." The cigarette dangling from his mouth bobbed up and down as he answered. "It was the one with the walnut stock, right?"

"Yeah, yeah, that's the one," answered Jimmy. His patience was all but gone.

"Well," Allan said and then hesitated once more. "I'm sorry, son; but someone else must have bought it."

Jimmy paled as his father's words registered in his mind and all at once his anticipation came to a disappointing end. Emotionally crushed, he dropped his head and gave a couple more discouraging thrusts to the bill of his cap.

"Relax, Jimmy. I'm only kidding!" Allan gave his son a few playful pokes to his ribs. "I bought the last one...you little knucklehead." Jimmy perked up immediately. For a brief moment, he'd thought his life was over.

When Allan pulled the carrying case from behind the seat of his Jeep, Jimmy was overjoyed. After all the waiting and dreaming, he now had his very own twenty-gauge shotgun. Allan removed the gun from its hard-shell case and handed it over to his glowing son.

"Well, what do you think?"

Jimmy cradled the gun while trying to determine if the moment was real. He looked up at his father and produced a tender, monumental smile. This ceremonial exchange was like no other for the boy. Staring down at his gun, Jimmy realized the importance of what was happening. From this moment on, things would be different. Because now, he held the highest of all bragging rights over each and every one of his buddies at school. This gun was sure to spur some jealousy among any group of nine-year-old boys. However, as important as that was to Jimmy, it did not compare to the gun's real significance. Jimmy held in his hands the one object that would ensure him the freedom for which he had been waiting all summer. This new twenty-gauge shotgun granted him with his own means to track down and harvest those furry-tailed squirrels.

He had heard his father boast of his successful hunting adventures time and time again. And come morning, Jimmy had great aspirations of doing the same or even better. He had participated in a few hunting excursions in the past, but never toting a gun of his own. Jimmy had also fired guns before—just like the one he was holding now—but usually at nothing more than plastic jugs and paper targets. For Jimmy, this was the big time.

That night, sleep did not come easily for Jimmy. He tossed and turned thinking of the grand hunting adventure and finally having his very own gun. When the alarm clock rang at 4 a.m., Jimmy sprang from his bed. Allan, who had awoken an hour before, was drinking coffee, puffing on a Winston, and watching the early news programs. Sandra was also awake busily preparing breakfast for her two dedicated hunters.

"It's kinda windy out there this morning," said Allan as his son staggered into the living room. "It might be hard to hear them. They're calling for rain too."

"I don't care about all that," said Jimmy, rubbing the sleep from his eyes. "We'll still find those suckers."

"Yes, son, I'm sure we will. Now go ahead and start getting ready so we can head out in a few minutes."

Jimmy needed no more persuading. After a delicious breakfast of scrambled eggs, toast, and bacon, he and his dad were out the door with their gear loaded in the Jeep and heading down the road. The ride to the local wildlife refuge seemed to take an eternity for the anxious lad. With his gun by his side, Jimmy sat listening to the high, lonesome sounds of his dad's country-western radio station. He daydreamed about having a successful hunt, one concluded and celebrated with a bagged limit of five squirrels each. He had seen his dad accomplish such a feat many times before and he was sure he could do the same.

"You think we'll see anything?" asked Jimmy.

"I don't know...maybe," answered Allan after taking a sip from his coffee mug.

"I hope so."

"So do I, son...so do I."

Jimmy and his father pulled in at the refuge around 5 a.m. and Allan began briefing his son.

"When we get in there and settled in, you'll have to be quiet the whole time. If you make any noise, you'll scare them away." Jimmy knew the protocol, but still listened carefully. "Keep your gun unloaded until we hear or see something. Soon as we locate one...well...you know what to do after that."

"Yeah, I remember," Jimmy assured his father with gleaming confidence.

Donned in their camouflaged hunting attire, the two started by hiking down a logging road that Allan had traveled many times throughout his years of hunting. Father and son walked side by side. Allan chose the left side and Jimmy walked on the right. The pair trekked a hundred yards deeper into the woodlands and selected a large beech tree to rest and wait under.

Sitting next to his dad, the young hunter tried to take notice of his surroundings. *The key to being a good hunter is observing,* Jimmy remembered his father's advice. The sun, however, remained hidden behind the horizon, which caused poor visibility throughout the forest.

The early morning winds subsided and Jimmy was captivated by the sounds of the waking wilderness. The tree frogs chirped messages back and forth. The morning songbirds were waking one by one. Their brief melodic solos rang sweetly, high above in the hidden treetops. Jimmy heard the thunderous jack-hammering of a redheaded woodcock pounding away on a defenseless tree. The natural sounds were all around and the forest was proudly coming to life.

As the pair sat, they watched as the sun rose above the Earth's horizon. It was not long after and the morning air became hot and thick with humidity. The sunlight peeked through the natural canopy from high above, revealing the vastness of the forest. Jimmy scoured the openness, but not a squirrel in sight.

"Now what?" he asked, turning to his father.

"We'll wait here a little longer," Allan whispered. "They should be up and moving about soon."

They waited and waited, but not a squirrel anywhere. Jimmy's focus soon moved from hunting to the harassing mosquitoes. The little bloodsuckers swarmed ferociously, buzzing all around, trying to feast upon his face, ears, and neck. He slapped, swatted, and scratched as red welts began to surface upon his exposed skin. Allan was able to keep the flying rascals at bay with a prevailing exhale of cigarette smoke. After seeing his son tormented by the annoying mosquitoes, Allan decided that he and Jimmy should try their luck elsewhere. Scratching fanatically, the boy followed his dad as they ventured deeper into the woodlands.

It was then the persistent hiking became strenuous for the young, adventurous hunter. His
hunting attire was soon saturated with sweat in the lingering heat. Jimmy's camouflaged hat had accuired a noticeable wet ring on the bill while his soggy pants clung to his legs, making it almost impossible to slip comfortably through the forest. The road, which initially was flat and straight, became a hilly trail of hell. This hunting adventure was not the one for which Jimmy had planned.

Hiking up a steep incline, Allan turned to his lagging son. "Are you gonna make it? You're looking a little peaked."

Jimmy was feeling whipped and beat down, but he would never confess that particular truth to his father. His flushed cheeks radiated as he cradled his new gun. He looked down to the Remington, searching for a spark of inspiration. He then looked back up to his father.

"I'll be fine," said Jimmy.

Allan grinned and then answered, "Okay, son."

A few steps later, Jimmy's dad spoke again. "This is a good spot right here. I've seen them in this area many times. We'll stop for a bit and see what happens." The only thing the boy could do was give an exhausting nod.

The rest was refreshing, but it allowed Jimmy's mind to wander. He tried to remain focused, but now, it was almost impossible.

He thought of school starting back and entering the fourth grade in the coming weeks. *Which teacher will I get? I hope it's not Mrs. Penn. She has to be the meanest teacher in school.* Jimmy's mind shifted to the camping trip he and his family had taken over the summer. *That was a big bass mom caught. It almost pulled her in. Good thing—*

"Did you hear that?" asked Allan.

"Hear what?" Jimmy asked, returning from his reverie.

Allan nodded to the left. "Over there."

"I don't hear anything." He did detect a few rumbles of thunder in the far distance.

"I think we got company, Jimmy boy."

The big moment was finally here. Jimmy pulled his focus together and with persisting effort he too heard the bustling of a woodland squirrel. The rattling of the tree limbs sent his heart racing out of control. However, his stirring mind went blank. He had been instructed earlier in the truck, but was not sure of what to do next.

"Load your gun, Jimmy...but slowly and quietly," Allan whispered.

He proceeded to do as his father said and carefully broke down the single shot twenty-gauge. With his trembling hand, he removed a shell from his front vest pocket and slid the cartridge into the gun's chamber. Jimmy then quietly closed the barrel back to its original position, and he and his father stood up slowly and waited.

Jimmy's anticipation was growing and his heart continued to race uncontrollably. He scanned the treetops with determination. He could hear the lively critter, but could not see it wandering about. He worried that his only chance at making a shot was going to pass him by.

The fear of going home empty handed ended quickly when Jimmy finally spied the furry squirrel scurrying gracefully back and forth on an oak tree limb about seventy yards away. He waited for further instructions. Allan thumbed in the squirrel's direction, signaling his son to proceed onward.

The distant thunder heard moments ago was moving in and the wind began blowing in heavy gusts. The tree limbs propelled wildly, which made keeping an accurate account of the furry tree climber more difficult for the young hunter.

After a few steps, Jimmy stopped behind a hickory tree and again scoured the treetops. His heart pounded as large, round beads of sweat formed across his brow. He swiped his forehead with his sleeve, looked about once more, and then carried on with his hunting pursuit.

In between heavy blasts of wind, the woodland squirrel came into Jimmy's sight once again. He discovered the critter perched on the side of a large oak tree, raking on a hickory nut, and flapping its tail. A surge of adrenaline coursed throughout the young man's small body.

Jimmy was about sixty yards away now and in desperate need of closing the gap as quietly as possible. Allan stayed behind and watched from a distance. Jimmy turned to look back and, with a nod, Allan signaled for his son to continue.

Jimmy's heart was pumping like never before. He looked at his surroundings and tried to determine the most efficient approach. He gazed to his left where he found a thicket of briar bush, which he knew trying to maneuver through would be hopeless. He then peered to the right where he discovered sparse undergrowth and a fallen log. His worry was steadily growing and he determined the second option would have to do.

Accompanied by a steady drizzle of rain, the wind now blew in constant blusters. As he battled the elements, Jimmy semi-circled in the direction of the oak tree, stopped within thirty yards, and now stood at a comfortable shooting distance and a promising view. He observed the tree with a keen and careful eye while his heart continued to beat like a timpani drum. No longer frolicking about, the critter had moved from the spot that Jimmy had seen it in earlier, and again his young mind raced with both eagerness and worry.

After another quick scan, Jimmy pinpointed the flapping of a bushy tail. The squirrel had moved much higher up and off to the right of the tree, perching itself on a skyscraping limb. Jimmy feared that his shooting skills could not accommodate such a challenging shot, but he had to try. He could not give up now.

With everything riding on this big moment, Jimmy intuitively squared his body. He set his feet, taking his shooter's position, just the way his father had taught him. He slowly brought his new Remington up to his right shoulder and pointed the long barrel into the high tree loft. After pulling back the hammer, he swayed the barrel only for a few moments before he carefully brought the woodland creature into the sights of his gun. He squinted as sprinkles of rain bounced steadily off his face. He pulled in a deep breath, held it, and gently squeezed the trigger.

The blast bellowed throughout the forest, sending many birds fleeing in all directions. The gun's deafening discharge produced an instant ringing in Jimmy's head and the powerful recoil jolted him back a few steps.

"Nice shot, Jimmy boy!" Allan shouted as the squirrel fell to the ground. "Nice and clean. I knew you could do it. Go ahead and pick him up and throw him in your vest. We'd better get out of here. This storm is picking up fast."

"Okay," was the only word Jimmy managed. The young boy was overwhelmed with joy and self-confidence.

"Dang, son. Wait 'til your mom hears about this...and your buddies at school!"

Allan continued to dote on his son as they began their long hike back to the Jeep. Neither the rain nor the hilly road troubled the young boy on the return trip. Instead, the two hunters laughed and joked as they always had. Along the way, Allan gave his son a few trademark pokes to the ribs and Jimmy returned a few of his own. The boy now felt like a real hunter, dignified in a way, just like his dad.

*

In Jimmy's mind, he has no problem visualizing that wonderful day which happened so many years ago. Though, the recollection stops when he hears his mother's voice.

"Jim," Sandra Harrison softly speaks. "Hey...Jimmy."

"Yeah...sorry," he answers, returning from his daydream while his mind skips back to his parents' living room.

"The minister is here."

Jim Harrison turns in his father's reclining chair. His heart beats rapidly, just as it did the morning of that memorable hunt so many years ago. Except now, he sits by his father's side hoping, praying, and believing the angels will spare his life a little while longer.

He watches as his father's chest slowly rises and falls. Allan Harrison's large, calloused hands, now skeletal in appearance, rest gently at his sides while his dying body lies peacefully in the contentment of his own bed. The cancer had spread viciously throughout the 70-year-old man's body.

Sandra Harrison, looking frail and tired, sits on the opposite side of the bed from Jim. She takes her husband's hand and places it into her own. She begins to gently rub and caress, hoping to induce some kind of reaction from the man whom she has loved all her life. She gazes down with anticipation, but there is no use. The old man is overloaded with pain medication and unresponsive.

Jim continues to watch his father's chest as it struggles to inhale and then exhale. He waits and anticipates the inevitable. With one last, laboring breath, Allan's chest moves no more. Jimmy circles around the bed to comfort his crying mother.

While looking down at his father, Jim realizes it's not sorrow that he's feeling, but an overwhelming sense of pride and honor. As he wipes away one lonely tear from his cheek, he begins to realize how lucky he is that a great man like Allan Harrison was his father and his friend.

~~~

The Good Neighbor

Peter Hughes lathered the final corner panel on his '68 Camaro. Washing this car, his most prized possession, was his duty, which he did at least once a week. Besides his outdated house, with the peeling paint, warped window frames, and cracked and slanted sidewalks, the car was the only item of any importance that Peter had been able to keep in that painstakingly drawn-out divorce. He had asked for nothing else.

He swirled his sponge and wiped while soapsuds slid down his scrawny forearm, covering the small name that he'd had tattooed there a few years ago. *Valerie*, a name he intended to have removed by laser surgery whenever he could save up the money.

With the garden hose, he rinsed the foamy water and exposed the car's shiny canary-yellow finish. Stepping back, he admired his baby as the last of the evening sun danced and paraded over the contours of its flawless body.

Perfection once again, he thought.

Soon after, his admiration for his car was interrupted when his neighbor, Guy Fickly, torqued the throttle on his new Harley-Davidson. From dual, chrome tail pipes black smoke bellowed, crossing the street and drifting toward Peter and his freshly washed car. The engine screamed and thundered throughout the usually quiet neighborhood.

Peter had enjoyed that rumbling engine for the first day or two. The sound had made his adrenaline rise, and he almost considered buying a bike for himself. He'd pictured cruising on the open road without a care in the world, enjoying the fresh country air and the freedom that he felt he sorely deserved.

But now, he scoffed every time he heard that blaring pain in the ass. He despised the noise more than he despised his cheating ex-wife. When Guy had bought the bike one week earlier, the roar of the engine could be heard at any time of the day or night. On most nights, Peter would lie in his bed and hopelessly clutch his pillow around his head trying to mute the chaos from across the street. Through his scarcely insulated walls, he heard wrenches clanking, Guy's cussing, and the engine revving to its highest rpms.

Now, eyes puffed and dark from smoke and lack of sleep, Peter stood in his front yard, breathing in the black cloud, glaring in Guy's direction. His first thought was to get his 12 gauge Remington from beneath his bed and put the mechanical monster out of its misery. He found much glory in this idea, but a more subtle approach would have to do for now. He dropped the sponge in the wash bucket and tossed the garden hose aside. He grabbed two Coors Lights from his ice chest, which sat on the cracked, slanted sidewalk, and took out across his yard and the road into Guy Fickly's driveway.

Walking up, Peter noticed the countless cigarette butts discarded over the newly blacktopped driveway.

A disgusting habit, he thought. When Guy saw Peter approaching, he cut the engine.

Guy was a shorter, stockier individual who had a rough-edged look. He had a buzzed haircut and scruffy beard and was probably a person you would want on your side if a barroom brawl broke out.

"How's it goin', neighbor?" said Guy.

"Going well," said Peter, showing his cordial side even though he wanted to lash out. "Come to check out this new beast of yours." He fought his way through the cloud of lingering black smoke.

"Yeah, always wanted one," said Guy. "Thought, what the hell, I ain't gettin' any younger. So, I just went out and bought the son of a bitch." Peter handed one of the beers to his neighbor. "Thanks, Pete."

Peter nodded. He cracked open the tab and then took a drink while circling the machine to get a better look.

"Sure is a beauty. What year is it?" he said.

"Ninety-five," said Guy. "She'll get down the road screamin' like a banshee. You wanna take 'er for a spin?"

Peter thought on the matter, and was tempted, but instead said, "No, better not. Already had a few too many suds today." He didn't want to appear hypocritical, especially with what he was about to say.

"Yeah, better not then," said Guy.

Peter swigged from his beer, cleared his throat, and said, "Hey, Guy, I hate to be the one to say this, but a lot of people are starting to complain about the noise you're making with this thing."

He had lied, but was sure the other neighbors had to find the noise as disturbing as he did. He assumed they were probably too intimidated by Guy's burly swagger to bring up the issue directly. Although, he couldn't blame them. Guy was a scary-looking sort whose bad side you probably didn't want to be on.

Guy popped the top of his can, took a healthy drink, and squatted beside his motorcycle.

"Hell, Pete," he said. "You know I don't give a damn about what people think of me. Besides, I'm just tunin' 'er up. A man has to take care of his equipment. You know that better than anyone." He set his beer on the driveway and grabbed a spark plug off an oily rag. He then grabbed the ratchet that was lying next to the bike's front wheel.

Peter scratched his head. He wasn't expecting Guy's response to be so logical. He couldn't rightfully argue with someone who was only trying to maintain his equipment.

"I wasn't saying you shouldn't take care of your bike, Guy. But you know how easily annoyed old man Baker becomes over everything." With a nod of his head, Peter gestured to the house next door to Guy's. "It's probably just a matter of time before he starts complaining to Town Hall, or goes to some other extreme."

Guy made the last turn of his ratchet, grabbed his beer, and stood.

"I'd like to see that old geezer try somethin' stupid like that. Next time his damn cat comes over and confuses my flower bed for a litter box, I'll send it home screamin' with a pellet in its ass."

Maybe mentioning old man Baker had been a bad idea. Peter didn't want to start trouble. He was only trying to make life a little easier for himself. He took another drink from his beer.

"There's something else," he said.

"What's that?" said Guy. "Ferguson runnin' his mouth too?" He was clearly irritated, and now looking toward the house of his other neighbor, Clive Ferguson.

The thought of unintentionally starting a neighborhood civil war crossed Peter's mind. "No-no, it's not that," he said almost in a panic. "It's just...well...I'm having trouble sleeping at night with all that noise you're making."

Tensing, Peter waited for Guy's response.

"Hell, Pete, why didn't you say that in the first place? I don't have a problem workin' in the daytime." Peter felt relieved by his answer, until Guy said, "Except it's a hell of a lot cooler at night, you know."

Damn it. He's right again, thought Peter. The days had been blistering hot, and he couldn't blame Guy for wanting to work in the cooler night air. He'd also remembered Guy's mild stroke last summer. He thought a bit longer and took another pull from his beer.

"Well, you shouldn't work in the heat, Guy. That could be dangerous."

"Hell, I'm too ornery to die," he said. "But I hear what you're sayin'. I'll try to cut the evenin' a little shorter from now on."

"That'd be great," said Peter, surprised by Guy's answer.

"But I'm only doin' it for *you*. Not for that old bastard over there." Guy pointed and emphasized with the end of his ratchet to old man Baker's house. "Or Ferguson, either."

"I sure do appreciate it, neighbor," said Peter.

"Not a problem," Guy replied. "Not a problem at all."

That night, Peter stared happily at the mirror while he brushed his teeth. He felt relieved knowing he was on the brink of getting a restful night's sleep. Tonight, there would be no engines blaring, no clanking wrenches, and no loud, thoughtless cursing.

He spat, wiped his mouth, and proceeded to the soft pillow top mattress and sat on the edge of his bed. He longed for vivid dreams and restful slumber. He knew he wouldn't meet the morning with contempt and despair as before. Instead, he would rise vigorously and full of joy.

He kicked off his house slippers, slid comfortably under his cover, and reached to push the switch on his reading lamp. There would be no reading tonight. Peter was prepared to reach that golden state of blissful rest and relaxation.

He lay peacefully, hearing only the soothing sounds of the chirping crickets outside his open window. A breeze slipped through the window screen, cooling his face, and he formed a gratified smile. He sank deeper into the mattress' thick cushion, expecting his mind to drift away at any moment. Not long now, he knew, and off to sleep he would go.

While nestled in his blankets, Peter's mind drifted away. But soon after, a violent stagger of kick-drums and distorted guitar-riffs penetrated the walls, causing his heart to bounce and skip. He rose, panting, grabbing his chest.

"Goddamn it!" he blasted. He stretched his arm and fumbled for the switch on his reading lamp. He slung off his cover, stood, and marched to the other bedroom window, pulling apart the blinds, and stared with crazy eyes toward Guy's lighted garage.

"What's wrong with these fucking people?" he said.

Guy's son, Austin, and his garage band were playing their music again. The teenage boy and his band had intruded on Peter's sleep on more than one occasion. Peter had talked to Guy about the blaring noise, and he thought they had come to a reasonable understanding.

"No problem, Pete," he remembered Guy saying. "I'll take care of it. Won't happen again."

Enraged, Peter spied through his blinds. And through the small rectangular window of Guy's garage, he could see Guy's greying, buzzed head keeping to the beat of the music.

Peter jerked his hand away causing the vinyl slats to slap back to their original position. He couldn't understand why Guy would let this happen again. Maybe this was spiteful turn play for his request to stop the roaring motorcycle engine. No matter. It was late and Peter would have to deal with this another time.

The next morning Peter arose with heavy stubble on his face and chose to bypass his usual shower and shave. He ambled to the kitchen to make coffee, and then to the corner of the living room where his desk and laptop awaited. He didn't feel very productive, but the deadline for his advice column loomed.

The keys of his laptop clacked as his article began to take shape. If anything could distract his mind, his writing could. Whether trying to steer some helpless soul out of depression or advise would-be college students on the importance of an education, this job was rewarding to Peter.

He typed away until a sequence of stern knocks on the door pulled him from his writing muse. He opened the front door and discovered a smiling, bright-eyed Guy Fickly staring back.

"Mornin', Pete," he said, puffing a cigarette.

"Good morning, Guy," Peter half grumbled. Unlike him, Guy appeared fresh and lively.

"Wonderin' if I could still borrow those posthole diggers?" he asked. "Goin' to start on that fence in the back yard."

With jaw clenched, Peter held onto his diminishing composure.

"Yeah—sure," he said. "Meet me around by the side door."

"Okay," said Guy.

In the hot, unventilated garage, Peter shuffled around bags of aluminum cans he'd been saving, bypassed a garden tiller, and scooted aside a few totes that were full of his ex-wife's belongings. Not only was his intrusive neighbor annoying him, but he also felt an old, unsettling rage stirring deep inside. He had phoned Valerie multiple times telling her to come and get her totes, and the rest of her stuff. He became infuriated every time he had to move the damn things to get to something he needed. And this time was no exception.

Eight more of Valerie's totes were stacked in the corner. Behind the stacks were the posthole diggers that Guy needed for his new fencing project. One by one, Peter lifted the heavy totes from the stack and placed them on the garage floor. He grabbed another, but his hand, now sweaty, slipped from the handle and the container's sharp, plastic lid scraped down his arm and the corner struck him in the chin. He went down, toppling over the other totes and onto the bags of aluminum cans.

Jutting his jaw, he checked its hinging motion, and when nothing seemed dislocated or broken, he scrambled back to his feet, cussing. Peter grabbed the posthole diggers, and a few moments later, he met Guy at the side door.

"Here," said Peter while beads of sweat ran down his brow and into his eyes. Again, he opened and closed his jaw.

"Thanks, Pete. I really appreciate it. I'll bring 'em back as soon as I'm done."

"No hurry," said Peter, wiping the sweat from his eyes.

"You really are a good neighbor," said Guy. "There ain't too many people like you left in the world."

"No big deal, really," said Peter, still blinking the sweat away.

"What's the matter? Get somethin' in your eye?" asked Guy.

"Just a little sweat."

Peter wiped his eyes again. He remembered the loud music that kept him up most of the night and early into the morning.

"That's quite the band your son has," he said.

"Thanks," said Guy. "I really think they have a lot of potential."

Yeah, the potential to drive someone bat shit crazy, Peter thought.

"The drummer, he's a little subpar, but learnin' fast," Guy continued. "They didn't keep you up last night, did they? I tried sound-proofin' the garage."

Peter said, "It *was* pretty loud."

"Damn, Pete. Sorry about that. It's just…well…they don't have anywhere else to practice. They're only tryin' to get better. They could be out vandalizin' shit or stealing cars—or somethin' worse."

"True," said Peter. "But maybe they could turn down the volume some."

"Sure thing, neighbor. And thanks again." Guy headed back across the street, slinging the posthole diggers up and onto his shoulder.

Inside, Peter grabbed a paper towel from the kitchen and wiped his sweaty hands and face. He then settled in front of his laptop and tried to lose himself once again in the sheer joy of his craft. He stared at the screen, but couldn't produce any words.

"You can do this," he muttered. "Just concentrate."

As his mind loosened and he forgot about his life's frequent annoyances, the words flowed freely onto the screen. While Peter made the final changes to his article, a series of yells came from outside. He got up and pulled the curtain on the front window and saw Guy's son, Austin, and a couple of his band mates riding skateboards up and down the road in front of his house.

In the middle of the street was a homemade ramp fashioned from a piece of ply board lying on a cement block. Each boy, one after the other, took the apparatus at full speed.

As he and his board landed perfectly on the street, Austin let out another ripping, celebratory scream and skated past Peter's driveway where he then maneuvered a sharp U-turn to fall back in line behind the other boys.

Next, Peter watched another boy zoom down the road, picking up speed, going faster and faster. When his wheels hit the ramp at an awkward angle, the boy and the skateboard went air borne, flying in opposite directions. Peter watched the kid land awkwardly on his side on the street, and the skateboard torpedoed through the air in an arching motion.

When the board landed, it hit one of the elevated cracks on Peter's slanted sidewalk where it toppled end over end until it smacked crudely against the passenger door of the mint '68 Camaro. Wasting little time, the boys gathered their skateboards and makeshift ramp and fled the scene.

Peter's heart fluttered and his face paled. He came close to vomiting. He was past the point of no return. This on going aggravation, this stirring rage, he could no longer contain.

Maybe I really should go get my gun, just say fuck it, and blow these bastards away. He went to the kitchen, grabbed a beer from the refrigerator, and thought the matter over.

He chugged his beer while trying to form these vile thoughts into more rational views. He tried desperately to see reason in all the torment he'd endured from his neighbor. Maybe Guy wasn't a peripheral thinker. Maybe he was unable to see the harm that he was doing.

Another burst of loud knocks lured Peter away from his soothing contemplation of an all-out neighborhood massacre. Repulsed, Peter's first thought was that one of the boys had come to confess the terrible catastrophe that they had committed. But instead, when he opened the door, he found a cheery Guy Fickly staring back, holding the spade end of the posthole diggers in one hand and the broken handle in the other.

"Afraid I had a little mishap, Pete," he said.

Peter flared. His eyes pierced and danced. "Is that so?"

"Startin' a little early, aren't we?" said Guy, noticing the beer in Peter's hand.

He took another gulp and shot back. "Sure, why not?"

Guy shrugged and said, "Well, I started diggin' and got down about a foot or so and the damn end snapped right off. Sorry, Pete. I'll pay you for the damage of course."

Peter didn't respond. His mind fogged over and he peered joyfully up to the beautiful morning sky. He smelled the wonderful aroma of freshly cut grass and heard the humming of old man Baker's riding lawn mower from across the street.

"You okay, Pete?" asked Guy.

Stripped away was his sanity. The long, restless nights were showing their ill effects on this once spirited and charismatic man. His engaging witticisms were no more and his striking handsome features had vanished as well. Peter had reached the end of the line.

"Sure, Guy. I'm fine," he said. "No need to pay me. I bought it at a yard sale for five dollars."

"Well, here, let me give you your five bucks back," said Guy, setting the handle down and reaching for his wallet in his back pocket.

"No, it's all right. Really."

Guy hesitated and said, "Pete?"

"Yeah?"

"Can I say somethin'?"

"Sure."

"I don't mean to sound like an ass, but maybe you should lay off the booze and try gettin' a little more sleep at night. You're lookin' a little run-down."

Peter snapped from his foggy realm. And just when he appeared to take offense, he cracked a smile. The smile broadened and morphed into a subtle snicker, and then a roaring laugh. Peter held up his beer and pointed to it, confirming Guy's take on his early morning drinking habits. But that wasn't the reason for his uncontrollable outburst. That wasn't the reason at all. It had come from the misguidance of an ignorant neighbor, unaware of the unspoken rules of how to be a good neighbor.

He laughed hysterically at a worried-looking Guy who stood on the front porch step holding the broken digging apparatus. Peter swung the door closed and lurched across his living room, set his beer on the end table, and sank onto the sofa. His laugh then changed to a deep, sorrowful cry, and tears streamed down his face. He fell over, burying his head into the sofa's cushion and cried until falling into a deep, delightful sleep, a sleep that he'd longed for, a sleep that had until now eluded him. He slept all day and night and didn't wake until the next morning, unbothered by man, woman, or neighbor.

~~~

Kate's Funeral

Kate sat calm and pleasantly content in the front row in one of the provided folding chairs. And even though she was attending her own funeral, she seemed unbothered by this small detail of not being alive. Instead, she looked around the large funeral parlor with the curiosity and fascination of a small child, one that has gone outside to discover nature for the first time. Except, this wasn't nature. This was death. This was Kate's death. The end of her physical being.

The old building, which had served for years as the town's funeral home, quickly filled with grievers of many kinds. Some of the people Kate hadn't seen since her early childhood. Some were former primary schoolmates; some were family members, high school friends, teachers, and other acquaintances. Through the crowded room, there was one face that she had yet to see, and for Kate, it was the face of an angel—her David. She carefully observed the parlor, looking all around, but again, she didn't see her love. She knew, though, it wouldn't be long, and he too would arrive to bid her a bittersweet farewell. She knew that for sure.

Two years before this day, the day of her funeral, Kate Longley met David Bennington when she was a freshman and he was a junior in high school. David played guitar in a garage band and was popular at their school. Kate loved music, and she also knew of David, but not on a personal level. That changed when they began sharing study hall together. It was then their relationship blossomed. Upon their first conversation, Kate had expressed to David her fascination for the arts—especially for the indie music scene.

"Indies are revolutionizing the industry," Kate had said, while sitting at her cramped desk, riddled with artwork of yesteryear's students. Smeared, inked images of rainbows, peace signs, and pot leaves graced the Formica surface.

"I totally agree," said David. He scribbled into a spiraled notebook. "It's like these big-wig record producers turn their noses up whenever someone mentions the words *independent artist*. I really don't get it. They need to open their eyes. This is the wave of the future."

"Absolutely," said Kate.

She stared into David's hazel eyes and thought he had the face of an angel. His artistic intellect also impressed her. The two carried on with their conversation a while longer, sharing their deep musical passions. David, after finding the nerve, asked Kate the question he had wanted to ask since their conversation had started.

Still nervously scribbling in his notebook, he said, "You know, if you're not too busy, maybe you could come by and watch us jam sometime?"

This had been what Kate was hoping for: a chance to hang out, a chance to get to know this person, who seemed to be more like her with each passing moment of their conversation.

"Sure. I would like that," she said, trying to contain a huge smile, but failing.

"Great," said David, grinning back. "You can come by tonight, if you want. We usually get started around six. I can give you directions."

"I know where it's at," said Kate. "I'll be there."

It had been the beginning of something wonderful. Thereafter, their love and devotion for each other grew as the young couple was together every waking moment. They would go to the library to read books, usually about art and literature or music and philosophy. Sometimes they would go to the classic movie theatre to see some of their favorite films from the golden age of cinema.

Several months passed and their relationship finally reached a level that assured Kate she would indeed spend the rest of her life with David, that she would someday marry him, someday become his wife. She couldn't wait for the day she would become Mrs. David Bennington.

As she reflected on those happier times among the living, reality struck Kate. *I'm dead*, she thought. It was then she realized that she would never get the chance to become David's happy bride.

Kate looked around the funeral parlor. She hadn't realized how much of an impact she had made on some of these people, the ones that loomed in the corner, chatting of how sad it was that a beautiful girl had died at such a young age, the ones that lingered in and out of the catering room eating the free mini sandwiches and drinking lemonade and iced tea. She had forgotten many of their faces over the course of her young life. Many wept as they walked by her open casket, and she almost became embarrassed the longer she watched them blubber over her chilled corpse.

"Quit crying, for God's sake," she said as another walked past her body. But the living couldn't hear the young and beautiful Kate Longley, and wouldn't hear her ever again.

Most did came to grieve for her, but there were some who came only to play witness to the almighty hand of death, which many thought sent one to the realm of the unknown. For Kate, death wasn't so bad. It wasn't a big deal, really. And now that she was deceased, she couldn't understand why the living had always made a big fuss over it.

From across the room, through the scattering of people, Kate noticed a man staring at her. She rose from the folding chair and turned in the man's direction. He stood casually, wearing a grey trench coat, hands in his pockets. Combed straight back, tight against his head, was his black, greasy hair.

Is he really looking at me? Kate thought.

"Can you see me?" She quietly mouthed the words, placing her pointed index finger to her chest. She repeated the question, but much louder, making sure this time the volume of her voice exceeded that of the annoying funeral score. The music was so depressing, Kate thought, and she wished she could've chosen the selection instead.

"Hey, come here," she said to the man across the funeral parlor. He was clearly staring in her direction. The man averted his eyes, pretending that he didn't notice Kate noticing him. He stepped out the parlor and headed down a corridor. Kate followed the man and watched him veer into another smaller room, the one designated for sitting and drinking coffee or tea and watching slide shows of the deceased.

When she rounded the corner of the door, going into the sitting room, Kate saw herself on a large, flat screen television that hung on the wall, above the fireplace. It was an image of when she was a toddler at Christmas time. In another, she posed with her first kitchen play set. The next one was a school picture of her when she was in the seventh grade, braces and all. These were nice memories, but she had no time to reminisce. She had to find this man and figure out why he was able to see her, the deceased her.

Kate looked around the room, but saw only the living, quietly chatting among each other. The man had vanished, or so she thought. She stood there more puzzled than ever. She had only been deceased for two days, and had already learned a great lesson about the afterlife. The lesson was that death could be as confusing, if not more so, as life. Kate was certain there was much more to know about death. Although for now, she wasn't sure of how she would learn those lessons. She walked out
of the sitting room and rejoined her family and friends, who continued to weep over her.

Standing up front by the casket, greeting the people who walked by giving their condolences, were Kate's mother, father, and little twin brothers. This was the first time she had seen them since she had passed, and it was indeed a sad sight. She loved her mother and father dearly, and even though they were at times nuisances, she adored her little brothers, Scotty and Steven.

Swabbing her crying eyes with a tissue, Kate's mother stood at the head of her daughter's open casket, probably hoping it was all nothing more than a horrible dream. Her father stood stone faced with his arm around his wife. Words had escaped him. He could do nothing more than give a simple nod as the people walked by. Little Scotty didn't cry much, and neither did Steven. However, at eight-years-old, they were of age to understand death, knowing that all this, this funeral, meant they would never see their big sister again.

Kate continued to look solemnly at her family. Again, for a brief moment, she forgot she was dead and said, "Don't cry, Mother. I'm all right." But Mrs. Longley couldn't hear her daughter and continued to cry, trying her best to greet the mourners as they walked by.

She kneeled down, becoming eye-level with her little brothers. "Everything's okay. Everything's just fine. I promise." She waited for a response, and again realized that they too couldn't hear her.

Kate stood and walked a few steps to the open casket where her physical body lay. She wore a black dress and in her ears were the pearl earrings that David had given her for her sixteenth birthday.

She said, looking back to her parents, "Why didn't you just cremate me? I look terrible. My nose is crooked and my entire face is swollen. Looks like I walked into a nest of hornets." The comment made her laugh. It was the first time she had done so since she had passed, and it relieved her. "Screw you, death. You're not so bad," she said. When she turned from her casket, she found herself nose to nose with the man who, earlier, had stared at her from across the room.

"Aaahh!" Kate screamed.

Huge, beady eyes looked at her, appearing to have no thought or feeling behind them.

She said, "So you can see me. I knew it!" The man said nothing in return and firmly held his gaze.

A few, short moments passed and still, the man stayed silent. He scowled, which struck Kate with fear.

She thought the worst had occurred, or was about to occur.

"You're not the devil, are you?" she asked with a tremble in her voice.

The man had been stoic with his burning gaze. But it was Kate's question that sent him bursting into a high-pitched laugh, which startled Kate again, causing her to retreat a couple steps in reverse until she bumped into her casket.

Through his laughter the man spoke. "Now that's a good one. I've never been accused of being the devil before!" He stuck out his hand. "No. I'm not the devil, kid. The name's Benny."

Reluctantly, Kate extended her hand.

Benny said, "My evil staring bit always gets quite the reaction from the newly departed. Usually, they go running off and don't return for a while."

Irritably, Kate said, "Ha ha. Very funny. Well, you could pass for the devil. You're evil looking enough—that's for sure."

"Relax, kid," said Benny. "Everyone gets pranked when they pass. Even I was pranked, although, it was more than fifty years ago."

"So, what are you doing here? And what do you want with me?" asked Kate, crossing her arms.

"Don't be so angry, kid. I'm here to help you. I'm your Afterlife Consultant."

Benny's title of Afterlife Consultant didn't register in Kate's mind. Instead, her focus gravitated toward the expense of such a service.

"Oh, that's great," she said. "So how much is *this* going to cost me?"

Saying nothing, Benny led Kate by her folded arms over into a secluded part of the funeral parlor—not that the living could hear their conversation, but sometimes a mortal habit such as this found its way into the afterlife. It was a common occurrence, even for someone who had been dead for more than fifty years, as Benny had been.

"Look, kid," Benny began. "Everyone gets assigned an Afterlife Consultant, and I happen to be yours. I'm here to help you, that's all. And it's not going to cost you a dime."

Kate saw the genuineness on Benny's face. She unfolded her arms and relaxed.

"But I'm not sure I even need a consultant. I mean, really. What's there to consult? I'm certain I'm dead. I don't need you to confirm that for me. This death and dying thing has been easy, really. Nothing to it." She flopped down onto a leather sofa that was next to her.

Benny stepped past the stubborn young girl, and sat down beside her on the sofa.

He said, "You're quite sure of yourself, aren't you? I have to admit you'd be the first person in the history of dying who truly knew what was going to happen in the afterlife. You have some big decisions to make, kid. And very little time to make them in."

Kate stared back up to the casket where her mother, father, and little brothers were still greeting the passersby. They seemed more distraught than ever. This tugged at Kate's heart, causing her dead self to feel grief, an emotion she hadn't experienced since her passing. Also, she peered around the room, looking for her David. And like before, her eyes did not find her angel-faced boyfriend.

"Okay, then," said Kate. "What do I have to do?"

"Come with me," said Benny, rising from the sofa.

Walking out of the parlor, Kate followed Benny back up the corridor and into the sitting room with the flat screen television and fireplace.

Making his way across the room, to the farthest corner, Benny stopped and stood in front of a wood-paneled wall, stained dark cherry.

"Hurry up, kid," said Benny. "We don't have much time. Your funeral will be over soon."

"I'm coming," Kate responded. "And quit calling me *kid*."

Benny stepped closer to the section of paneling, and with automated know-how, the wall slid from one side to the other. Although there was no sound made, Kate looked with worry behind her, hoping the living people in the sitting room hadn't noticed what was taking place. They continued to drink their tea and coffee, quietly chatting among each other.

A dingy stairwell, half-lit by a single burning bulb, disappeared down into a darkened cavern.

"I'm not going down there," Kate said nervously.

"Unless you want to end up a wandering soul with no direction, I suggest you follow me," said Benny.

Being a wandering soul with no direction didn't sound appealing to Kate. Benny stepped into the stairwell and she followed closely behind. The wood-paneled wall slid back to its original position.

The stairwell smelled like a musky basement or wine cellar. On both sides of Kate were water-stained cinder blocks that were a part of the old funeral parlor's foundation. When Benny came to the bottom step of the stairwell, he turned a dimmer switch and, in front of Kate, a room with which she was familiar lit up. As she entered the lighted area, there was no denying it; this room was indeed her family's living room.

"How'd you do that?" asked Kate.

"It's no big deal, really," said Benny. "We, the Afterlife Consultants, try to choose a comfortable setting for the newly departed. Also, some place where we won't be distracted."

"It's comforting, in a way," said Kate, looking around.

"Good. I'm glad you think so."

Benny settled in a leather reclining chair, and Kate took refuge on a large beanbag, that belonged to one of her twin brothers. She punched and manipulated the bag until she was lounging comfortably. Benny opened a satchel, which was already beside the leather reclining chair before they had arrived, and from it pulled the necessary documents.

"This is what I was telling you about," said Benny of the papers. "You have to decide what your afterlife arrangements will be."

"I'm not sure what you mean," said Kate.

Benny flipped to the third page of the bundle.

"You have to decide whether you want to stay in the land of the living and be a guardian angel to a friend or loved one or whomever you choose, or enter the Land of Eternal Bliss and say goodbye to everything you've ever known. It says it right here." Benny indicated with a pen to the specific section of the page.

Kate rose from the beanbag, grabbed the papers, and looked them over.

"The Land of Eternal Bliss doesn't sound like a place that's very *blissful*," said Kate.

"I don't know firsthand," said Benny. "That's what it's always been defined as. I've always worked here, among the living, first as a guardian angel, then as what you see now, an Afterlife Consultant.
Usually, though, we all find ourselves there, eventually."

Benny continued to ramble, explaining the particulars of being a guardian angel and entering the Land of Eternal Bliss—or at least what he thought he knew of it. Kate handed the papers back to Benny.

"You see," said Benny, "you have to make a decision very soon. When they close the lid on your casket, you forfeit your choice. Then, they'll assign you, at random, to be a guardian angel to some stranger or send you automatically to the Land of Eternal Bliss. So what's it going to be, kid?"

"Stop calling me *kid*."

"Err...sorry. What's it going to be, *Kate?* And please hurry. You must choose quickly."

The urgency in Benny's voice alarmed Kate. However, it took her only a moment to decide how she wanted to spend her time in the afterlife. She thought of her dear, sweet David.

"I choose my boyfriend," said Kate. "I want to be his guardian angel."

Benny's pale face was confused. "I'm afraid you can't choose him. You must choose someone else."

"But you said I could choose anyone I want," Kate sputtered. "And I choose David."

"Yes, of course. But that person has to be...you know...*living.*" The last word trailed off Benny's tongue, slowly, until it dwindled to a whisper. He then said, "You mean you don't know?"

"Know what?" asked Kate. "What are you talking about? And what do you mean...*has to be living?*" Her voice grew louder and she became impatient with Benny and the conversation.

"You don't remember, do you?" said Benny.

"Remember what?" she asked, throwing her hands in the air.

"Your wreck, kid."

"Of course I remember," she said. "How could I forget?" She went on to tell Benny about her car crash, the whirlwind of screeching tires and blinding headlights, not to mention the twisting sound of metal and the cloud of choking smoke. She paused, trying to recollect the entire event. She then said, "That's when that other blue SUV crossed the center line and hit us."

Kate abruptly stopped. When the word *us* was said aloud, a fleet of vivid images swarmed her memory and intense anxiety swept throughout her. It was then she remembered everything about that horrible night; it was then she remembered David, riding along in the passenger seat, holding her hand.

"Kate," Benny began, using a soft, understanding tone. "David passed away in that wreck, just the same as you. I'm sorry. I thought you knew. But you really must hurry and choose. They'll be closing your casket at any moment. I can hear them playing your farewell music up there now."

Kate said, "Well, what has David chosen? Maybe we can spend the afterlife together in the Land of Eternal Bliss."

"I don't know," said Benny. "Let me look." He pulled from his trench coat pocket some sort of electronic device. He scrolled and touched its digital pages until he came across the site he was looking for. Benny said, looking at the screen, "Says here he hasn't made his decision yet. It also says he has until tomorrow to do so." He put the device back into his pocket. "Sorry, kid, that's all I know."

Kate dropped her head and, in death, she cried. All through life she had made many choices for herself, some easy, some difficult, and as she was finding out, even in death there were difficult decisions to be made. Kate had experienced every human emotion possible.

She had known anger; she had known courage; and she had even known hate. Of course, she also had known love, the greatest emotion of them all.

And Kate loved her family, loved them dearly. As she sat there mulling over her dilemma, she found it silly and a bit shameful that she had never considered being a guardian angel for her little brothers. She wiped her tears and looked up to Benny, who sat in the reclining chair, nervously, with pen and paper in hand.

"Have you decided?" he asked.

Kate shifted some in the beanbag chair and said, "Yes, I have. I've decided to be the guardian angel for my little brothers, Scotty and Steven. I want to watch over them. They need me."

"That's an excellent choice," said Benny. "But I'm afraid you can choose only one."

"Only one?" said Kate. "But that's not fair."

"Sorry. Rules are rules."

She loved her little brothers equally. How was a decision like this to be made? She asked Benny, "If I choose one will I still get to see the other?"

"Of course," answered Benny. "And everyone he associates with throughout the rest of his life. You must choose now."

"Okay...okay, I choose...Scotty. No! Steven. This is so difficult. Why must I choose only one?"

"Sorry. Rules are rules," Benny said again.

"Okay, then. I choose Steven!"

Upon her decision and signing the document, the final note of her farewell song was played and, ultimately, the door on her casket was closed and sealed. Then, an unexplainable yet powerful blast of energy rushed through Kate's immortal soul. At that moment, she closed her eyes and all life's unanswered questions gained relevancy and understanding. No longer did she feel clueless, as she had been in her days as a mortal human being. No longer did she feel frightened or anxious, or sad or lonely, or fearful of what the future may bring. She felt wonderful. A pure and satisfying stream of joy and contentment. No worries. No doubts. It was a feeling that she had never felt before.

When Kate opened her eyes, the sight of the sun filled a blue sky up above. She felt the cool, prickly grass underneath her arms and hands. From her parents' front lawn, she rose and observed her two little brothers running and playing. She watched as they passed a football, wrestled, and rode their bikes up and down the street.

While she was keeping a particularly watchful eye on Steven, a figure walking up the sidewalk caught her attention. The young man idled up the driveway, across the yard, and flopped down on the grass beside Kate. He held a rose in his hand.

"I'm glad you're here," she said calmly.

"Me too," said David. He handed the rose to his girlfriend.

The reunited couple sat the rest of the afternoon watching the twin brothers and enjoying each other's company once again. Kate looked after Steven while David watched over Scotty. Two brothers. Two guardian angels.

~~~

Fading Jump Shot

Kent stepped to the free-throw line with two seconds remaining in his season-opening game at Spalding University. He had practiced shooting thousands of these shots. His team trailed by one. *No pressure*, he thought. *I got this.* The referee bounced him the ball, and he performed his usual routine: three dribbles, short pause, deep breath, and then release. The packed field house was all but silent as Kent's first shot arched through the air and found its way through the rim, sinking through the bottom of the nylon net. The Spalding fans cheered and the referee gathered the ball and signaled that only one shot remained.

No pressure, Kent thought again. *Just like in practice.* He dribbled three times, paused, and breathed deeply. But something didn't feel right, something in his chest. His heart fluttered. The flutter turned into a stabbing pain, one that overwhelmed the eighteen-year-old basketball prodigy. He dropped the ball, clutched his chest, and staggered a few steps toward his bench, toward
his coach and teammates, before collapsing onto the floor. The emergency medical technicians standing on

the sidelines wasted little time and rushed onto the court. The young man held his chest, as thousands watched from the stands with fear and worry on their faces.

Kent Weber loved the game of basketball. He played countless of hours year round, practicing, studying, and honing his skills. Everywhere he went he carried a basketball, almost as if it was a part of his being. It was his life, the reason he rose out of bed in the morning, this game called basketball.

Kent was tough, physically and mentally. The day he found out his parents were divorcing, his mental toughness was put through its biggest test yet.

"If you guys don't care about this family, why should I?" he said to his mother and father. They were having the sit-down talk that many parents have with their children when a divorce is looming.

"Don't be like this, Kent," said his father. "Our divorce has nothing to do with you. I promise, son."

"This has *everything* to do with me," said Kent. "I'm leaving for Spalding University in a couple months and you guys are bailing on me."

"We're not bailing on you, son," said his father.

"Your father is right," said Kent's mother. "We still love you and we'll both continue to support you."

Kent sprang up from his chair. "If you two don't care then neither do I."

"Kent, get back here!" his father demanded.

Kent didn't listen. He stormed across the living room, out the front door, slamming it behind him. He got into his pick-up truck, and squawked the tires in first and second gears, heading to his girlfriend's house.

Kent couldn't grasp why his parents were taking such drastic measures. Heartbreak and rage filled the young man. He felt duped by the people who were supposed to love him the most.

Arriving at his girlfriend Jennifer's house, Kent explained his parents' approaching divorce. Jennifer listened intently as he vented his frustrations.

"It sucks, you know," said Kent. "I'm so used to everybody being there in the same house. I'm sure my dad will get his own place soon."

Jennifer said, "My parents get along way better now that they're divorced. And what's weird is they act way cooler toward me." She paused, noticing her words weren't reaching her troubled boyfriend. She then said, "At least graduation is over. Now we can party all summer—until you go to college anyway. That'll take your mind off things."

"Maybe," said Kent. He sat on the edge of Jennifer's bed, slumped over, elbows on knees, looking at the floor in a daze.

Jennifer sat down beside him. "I'm going to miss you when you're gone. We should really make the most of this summer." She gingerly laid her head onto Kent's shoulder.

Kent said, "Maybe I won't go."

"What do you mean?" asked Jennifer.

"To college. Maybe I just won't go. That'll teach them."

Jennifer pulled her head from Kent's shoulder. "Baby, you need to relax. That's crazy talk. This is your future you're talking about."

"So what. They don't care," he said of his parents.

"Yes, they do," said Jennifer. "Just relax." She rummaged through her purse which was sitting beside her on the bed. "Let's smoke this," she said, holding a huge joint in her hand. "It'll make you feel better."

Kent shook his head. "You know I can't smoke weed. It makes me paranoid."

Jennifer thought for a moment and then laid the joint on her nightstand beside her bed. She opened the nightstand drawer, and pulled out a small plastic baggy filled with an illuminating yellow substance and a razor blade.

She said, "You want to do a line instead?"

Unlike the joint, the baggy snared Kent's attention. He had actually tried this yellow substance, known as methamphetamine, about a month before while at a party. The person who had turned him on told him that it would give him the power to out-shoot, out-rebound, and out-run anyone on the court. He vividly recalled that night and remembered the incredible feeling the drug had given him.

"Sure, if you want to," he said.

"I always want to," said Jennifer.

"I didn't know you were into this stuff."

"I like it every now and then," said Jennifer.

From the wall, Jennifer removed a picture and set it down between them. On its glass top she dumped a small mound of the yellow powder and carefully chopped it with the razor blade, forming two small lines, symmetrical in size. She rummaged through her purse again and pulled a stub of plastic tubing, about the diameter of an ink pen. Jennifer snorted her line, and handed the plastic tube to Kent.

Identical to the first time he'd sniffed the powder, a wicked burn bore through Kent's nasal cavity, which led to an electrifying sensation of both pain and pleasure. He fell back on the bed, eyes watering. Only a few moments passed before the drug's real effect started to bounce around inside his head. He wiped his watery eyes and smiled.

"Wow. That's more like it," he said, sniffling and with spirit steadily rising. "I wish I had more of that."

Jennifer fell back on the bed beside her boyfriend. "There's some left in the baggy."

"No, I mean a whole lot more—whenever we want it," explained Kent.

"Baby, I can get all you want."

"Really?" Kent brushed at his nose with his fingers and sniffed again.

"Absolutely," said Jennifer. "All I have to do is make a phone call."

"You think I could meet your dealer?"

Jennifer hesitated. She then said, "I'm not sure. He's particular with who he meets. He's funny like that."

"But I'm your boyfriend. If he's cool with you, he'll be cool with me."

"Maybe," said Jennifer. "But I'll have to talk to him first."

She began kissing Kent's neck about the same time the drug's effect boosted into overdrive. With feelings of grandeur, Kent had little doubt that this was going to be a great summer after all. With his girlfriend beside him and the incredible high he was feeling, he had all but forgotten the bad news of his parents' divorce.

A couple days later, his father moved out and after that, Kent avoided going home as much as possible. On most nights, he would sneak through Jennifer's bedroom window and crash with her. The young couple was together regularly, mostly occupying their time by delving into a bag of the finest meth that Jennifer scored from her dealer.

One night while Kent and Jennifer were doing their usual routine of snorting lines in her bedroom, the conversation again came up about the drug dealer.

"Have you talked to him?" asked Kent with a hint of annoyance.

"Talked to who?" she asked.

"Your connection."

"Not yet," she said, bent over, holding a stub of a drinking straw to her right nostril.

"When?" he asked, still annoyed.

Jennifer's face contorted and her eyes watered as the power rocketed through her nasal cavity. "Soon, baby. Just relax. I'll set it up soon."

"That's what you keep saying, but it's not happening."

"These things take time," she said.

"Yeah, but I'm leaving in a week."

"Don't worry, baby, it'll work out."

"I doubt it," said Kent.

Jennifer knew getting Kent high and having a good time was one thing, but bringing him to meet her dealer was another. She then remembered a party that was happening across town. She mentioned the party to change the uncomfortable topic.

"Sure, let's go," said Kent. His eyes were wide, his pupils expanded, and he was ready to party. He felt like an invincible king and Jennifer was his fair maiden queen.

Parked out on the street in front of the party house, they heard the music playing. They both snorted another line while sitting in the car. When they got inside, several people—close to fifty, Kent estimated—stood around the large, two-story home, dancing, drinking, and passing around joints. Kent didn't smoke weed, but he liked the smell. Whether sweet or skunky, it didn't matter.

"I'm gonna go find some beer," said Jennifer loudly so Kent could hear her over the music.

"Sure, okay," said Kent, yelling back. "I'm gonna hang out in here."

"Okay," she said, and walked away through the crowded room.

Feeling energized, Kent waited only a short while before he too wandered through the sea of people. The six foot five inch basketball star towered over most of the other partygoers. Many
people nodded as Kent walked by. Some even greeted him by name, recognizing him as the local basketball hero.

"What's up, Kent," one person said loudly over the music. Not knowing the person, Kent nodded and said hello. He walked a little further when another person said, "Hey. It's Kent Weber. How's it going?"

"Hey," Kent said, turning to a muscled kid wearing a tight, black t-shirt. Kent didn't know him either, but the kid seemed genuinely nice.

"Ready to light it up for Spalding U?" the kid asked, gesturing a fading jump shot as Kent walked by.

"Totally," said Kent, smiling and walking on.

"Good luck, man," said the muscly kid.

"Thanks," said Kent.

Heading in no particular direction, Kent walked and sidestepped through the people until he arrived in a section of the house that wasn't as populated. He stopped and looked around, occasionally making small talk with a few people. Standing a short distance away was a girl, looking of Hispanic descent with long, dark hair, staring in his direction, smiling. Graciously, Kent nodded and smiled back.

It wasn't long before the girl scooted through the crowd and made her way over to the tall boy that she'd been admiring from afar.

"Don't you play baseball or something?" She tiptoed to speak and Kent bent over to listen. When he did, he gathered a large whiff of the girl's alluring perfume. "I've seen you somewhere," she said.

"I play basketball for North Central," said Kent. "I'm going to Spalding U in the fall. My name's Kent Weber."

By now, the meth that he'd snorted earlier in the car was at its peak and his heart thumped rapidly in his chest. Kent felt perspiration forming on his front and back, soaking through his t-shirt.

"So that's where I've seen you," said the girl. "You played against my brother, Felipe. I'm Nicole, by the way. Nicole Sanchez."

He pondered the name. *Felipe...Felipe Sanchez.* Kent knew the name. He played for the crosstown rivals Jefferson High. There had always been bad blood between the two high schools.

"Nice to meet you, Nicole." He sniffed and twitched his nose again. "But I don't think your brother is a big fan of me or my high school."

"Who cares what he thinks? He's an asshole." She noticed a bead of sweat that started at Kent's temple and rolled down the side of his baby-faced cheek. "You want to go outside where it's cooler?" she asked.

He looked back in the direction where he and Jennifer had separated moments ago. He didn't see his girlfriend.

"Yeah, sure. Lead the way."

Nicole led him to a sliding screen door that opened to the backyard. Large security lights mounted on both ends of the house lit the area where several people stood talking and laughing. Kent saw a group of people funneling beer. He and Nicole walked over to sit on a secluded picnic table, half in the shadows and half in the security lights' casting glow.

"So are you here by yourself?" asked Nicole. She scooted closer to the basketball star.

"All by myself," he said. "A friend told me about this party, so I thought I'd come by and check it out." He lied only to see what the girl's intentions were, although he had a good idea. He had no desire to be with her, and was only testing her, teasing her, and maybe flirting a little.

"I bet you've had lots of girlfriends," said Nicole.

"Not really," said Kent.

"I don't believe it. A big-time basketball player like you has to have been with lots of girls."

"Only a few," said Kent, striking a modest tone.

Nicole slid a little closer yet, and began rubbing Kent's inner thigh, leading further up his leg. As Kent was about to pull her hand away, he heard sprinting footsteps from behind, and shortly after felt a hefty smack to the back of his head.

The smack stunned Kent long enough so his attacker could get in front of him and throw a solid punch, which struck him squarely in his nose. Blood poured and Kent staggered to his feet trying to defend himself. Nicole jumped from the table and watched as her brother, Felipe, attacked the basketball star.

"Hit him, Felipe, hit him!" she cheered. The sexy temptress had done her part by luring Kent from inside the house. It was now up to her brother to finish the job.

Someone else yelled, "Fight!" and in seconds people flooded into the backyard to watch the action unfold. Another yelled, "Kick his ass, Kent!"

Finally, the bigger and taller Kent collected himself, reached out, and connected with a hard, straight jab to the right eye of Felipe Sanchez. The hit produced a loud popping noise that made some of the onlookers cringe. Kent then swung with a left cross that rattled Felipe across his jaw. Felipe tried to shake off the heavy blow. From beneath his eye was a wide gash from which blood oozed and rolled down his face. Once more he came at Kent, but stopped when he saw the stout, young man holding firm and ready to do battle, looking a bit crazy in the eyes. Felipe then signaled to someone in the crowd. He nodded in Kent's direction, and a giant of a boy emerged.

Coming from behind Kent, the boy subdued him with a rear choke, bringing Kent to his knees. Kent tried to break free by twisting and pulling at the thick forearm around his throat. He gasped for air while Felipe struck with another solid fist, this time to the mouth. Another cut opened and blood poured. Kent continued to squirm and tug at the forearm around his neck, but couldn't overcome the strength of the big boy.

Felipe looked on with a gratifying smirk. This time he reared back and landed a powerful kick to Kent's stomach. The kick jarred Kent's entire being and drained him of what little fight he had left. He no longer tugged at the forearm around his throat, but dropped his hands to his abdomen, grimacing in pain, still gasping for air.

The crowd had grown substantially and no one had yet stepped in to help the lop-sided matchup. Then, through the drunk and stoned partygoers burst the muscly boy who had spoken to Kent earlier. With a pair of beefy hands, the kid grabbed the boy giant by his own throat, causing his eyes to bulge and ultimately to let loose of Kent Weber.

With ease, the muscly boy slammed Kent's assailant to the ground where he kicked and pummeled the big boy. Many in the crowd winced at hearing sound after sound of thudding sneakers connecting with the big boy's ribcage.

Next was Felipe, who stood watching, too afraid to come to the defense of his accomplice. The muscly boy started in Felipe's direction, but the coward back pedaled a couple steps before turning and sprinting away, disappearing into the crowd. Nicole followed behind her brother.

On the ground with a bloody nose and mouth, Kent clutched at his stomach. His body shivered as a blast of shock set in. He tensed and let out a scream.

"It's cool, it's cool," said the muscly boy, trying to calm Kent. "He's gone." The other boy, holding his ribs, scrambled to his feet and also disappeared into the cluster of people.

Running to Kent's side was Jennifer. She screamed and dropped both the beers she held when she saw her boyfriend's battered face.

Kent huffed in and out through his nose and mouth, spraying a mixture of blood, saliva, and sweat. "I'm going to kill that son of a bitch," he said. He held his stomach and tried to stand.

"No!" Jennifer demanded. "Just sit here."

"Chill, Kent," said the muscly boy. "He's gone, bro. Wait to fight another day."

Kent stared with menacing eyes toward the direction in which Felipe Sanchez had run. He knew his day of revenge would come, but it wouldn't come soon enough.

The next day—after hearing her boyfriend grumble and complain—Jennifer finally set up a meeting and drove Kent over to her dealer for the first time. The dealer had also been insistent on convening with the basketball prodigy, although Jennifer hadn't mentioned that to Kent.

Kent was more than a little nervous about the meeting. And he hadn't slept any. On the way over, he played and fidgeted with the door handle, sun visor, and anything else he could put his hands on.

"So what's he like?" asked Kent through swollen lips. Both his eyes had also blackened extensively throughout the night and morning. He opened and closed the glove compartment door, and then repeated this action two more times.

"He's cool," she said, as she drove down the street that led to her dealer's home. "But you need to relax. He's liable to freak out by the way you're acting."

"I can't help it. I'm nervous and I need a fix," he said. "Maybe this was a bad idea. Maybe I should come back another time. Just let me out here on the curb."

The car pulled into a driveway that had two concrete lion statues on either side of it. Jennifer said, "It's too late for that. We're already here. And
I just saw someone pull the curtain on the window."

Unwillingly, Kent stepped out of Jennifer's car and followed her down a sidewalk, around the corner of the house, to the backdoor. After a soft peck of knocks, the backdoor opened, and a large, balding man who looked to be in his mid-forties greeted Jennifer and Kent. Wearing no shirt, the man exposed a thick covering of chest and shoulder hair. A gold chain hung around his neck and he wore black sweat pants with white sneakers on his feet.

"Jennifer! Baby girl! Come in. Come in," said the man. Jennifer and Kent stepped inside.

"Victor," Jennifer began, "this is Kent, my boyfriend."

"How you doing, Kent?" asked the man named Victor.

"Nice to meet you," said Kent. He put out his trembling hand.

Victor had a round face and a set of plump cheeks that pinched around a tiny nose. Noticing Kent's shakiness, he said, "Relax, son." He gave Kent's hand a firm squeeze. "I'm not going to hurt you. I'm a big fan. I've been watching you play since you were a freshman. You have talent." On his face he wore wire-rimmed glasses, over which he appeared to gaze, looking at Kent's battered face, although he said nothing about it.

"Thanks," said Kent. He breathed deeply, struggling to regain his usual composure. He and Jennifer followed Victor into another part of the house—the part in which Jennifer knew he normally conducted his business—and Kent noticed the man's back was equally as hairy as his chest and shoulders.

"Sit down, sit down," said Victor, motioning to the two high-back chairs in the corner of the room. The room had a bar that Victor sat next to on a leather-padded stool. It was then another individual walked into the room. "Kent, meet Cecil," said Victor.

"Hey," said Kent. The man named Cecil didn't acknowledge Kent or Jennifer and walked over to stand behind the bar behind Victor.

"Don't be offended, Kent," said Victor. "Cecil here doesn't talk much."

"I'm not offended," said Kent.

"Good," said Victor. He grabbed an empty tumbler from the bar and Cecil, who had already grabbed a bottle from the shelf behind him, poured straight Scotch into the glass. "I would offer you kids a drink, but I don't *contribute* to minors." Victor laughed at his joke and then sipped from his glass.

Jennifer said, "So how's business, Victor?"

The shirtless man took another drink from his glass and said, "Not bad. Not bad. But I don't want to talk business. Not right away."

"Sure. Okay, Victor," said Jennifer.

"So, Kent," Victor turned his attention back to the basketball star. "When do you leave for Spalding University?"

Instead of answering, Kent looked to the man named Cecil behind the bar. He had a flattop haircut and a set of thick mutton chop sideburns. He was an intimidating sort. Again, he stared at Kent and Jennifer, unflinching.

Under Cecil's steadfast gaze, and deprived of sleep, Kent squirmed and moved around in his seat. He needed a fix. He smacked his mouth a lot and looked back to Victor. His mind drew a blank as if all the words in his head had vanished.

Noticing her boyfriend's struggle to speak, Jennifer said, "He leaves next weekend."

"That's great," said Victor. He paused. Looking up, he appeared to search his own thoughts. "You know, I also played basketball in high school."

Kent looked at the large, balding man sitting at the bar with the tumbler of Scotch in his hand and had a hard time imagining that a man of his stature was once physically fit and able to participate in any type of sporting event.

"You could almost say I was pretty good," continued Victor. "But of course I pissed that away by falling into the wrong crowd. It's a shame so many young and talented kids fall prey to such nonsense. Wouldn't you agree, Kent?"

Kent tried to listen. His mind wandered again and he shifted nervously in the seat and smacked his mouth again, raking his tongue across his teeth. In a delayed response he said, "Yeah...it's a shame."

With his back turned to the bar and without looking, Victor placed his hand on the shiny, lacquered bar top behind him and tapped his fingers three times. Without speaking, as he had yet to do, Cecil reached down behind the bar and pulled out a large, square mirror that was equipped with a short straw and several lines of meth.

"Maybe this will help you relax," said Victor. He gave a glance to the young couple in the corner. With a head gesture, he invited them over to the bar.

Several hours had gone by since Kent and Jennifer had had their last fix. Kent's craving for the drug exceeded anything he'd ever experienced before. He wanted it. He needed it. He and Jennifer enthusiastically sprang from their seats and joined Victor at the bar. Victor slid the mirror across the bar top to the anxious couple.

Invigorated once again by the mere sight of the drug, Kent and Jennifer both snorted two lines each and waited as their spirits rose back to their comfortable and usual levels of euphoria.

"This is my best product yet," said Victor.

"How much?" asked Jennifer.

"The usual—hundred a gram."

"We'll take it," said Jennifer without hesitating.

Victor signaled to Cecil, and Cecil pulled a small plastic baggy from behind the counter. Jennifer counted out five twenty-dollar bills and scooted them over to Victor. Victor handed the baggy to Jennifer.

Victor finally asked Kent, "So who beat the hell out of your face? Somebody did a number on you, son."

Still fighting off the burning effects of the drug, Kent said, "Some punk named Felipe Sanchez. He ran away before I could really lay into him. He'll get what's coming to him. You can bet on that."

Victor said, "I could take care of it for you." He took another sip from his glass and set it back on the bar.

"What do you mean?" asked Kent.

"You know...rough him up a bit. Let him know he's messing with the wrong people. That sort of thing."

Jennifer turned to Kent with an almost panicked look on her face. Without speaking, she gave a piercing stare, trying to dissuade him from taking Victor's offer. She knew Victor's intentions. Known in the local drug ring as someone who lures in young, naïve teenagers with acts of kindness, Victor would recruit these kids and try to turn them into his drug runners, helping him spread his product, helping him build his empire. Jennifer had known a few kids who had worked for Victor. She remembered them eventually dropping out of school and becoming full-blown meth addicts. She didn't want that for Kent.

Kent sensed his girlfriend's concern, but he couldn't help thinking what a pleasure it would be to know that Felipe would indeed get a little taste of what he had dished out to him.

"I like that idea," said Kent.

"Great," said Victor. "I'll have one of my guys take care of it."

"Okay," said Kent. "But don't hurt him too bad. Just enough to get the point across."

"Don't worry, son, I always get my point across."

Annoyed that her boyfriend didn't heed her warning, Jennifer stepped down from her bar stool.

"We really should be going," she said insistently. "We don't want to waste anymore of your time." Victor and Kent also stood.

"It's been a pleasure as always," Victor said to Jennifer. She forced a meager, artificial smile. "And Kent, come back anytime. I'll be watching you at Spalding. You're going to do great things."

"Thanks," said Kent. He didn't show it, but he was all smiles from within, and it wasn't from the compliment. Now, he had the green light to an endless supply of drugs, which previously he could obtain only through his girlfriend. Victor showed them to the backdoor, and Kent and Jennifer left with drugs in tow.

The following Friday, the day before he left for college, Kent was home, upstairs, working out in his bedroom when he heard footsteps storming up the stairs.

"They got Felipe! They got Felipe!" yelled the voice he recognized as Jennifer's. She ran into his room.

"What the hell are you talking about?" said Kent, standing in the middle of his room, shirtless and sweating, holding a dumbbell in each hand.

Through heavy breaths Jennifer said, "Victor's guys...they got Felipe. He's in the hospital, on life support. I told you that was bad idea. Damn it, Kent, I told you!"

Kent set his dumbbells on the floor and said, "But I told Victor to take it easy on Felipe." He walked over, grabbed his shirt off his bed, and wiped the sweat from his face.

"I know, but he doesn't care what you have to say. He doesn't care what any one has to say.
Victor does what he wants, when he wants. Felipe may die."

"How do you know? Who told you?" asked Kent.

"I just know, Kent. Trust me. It happened, okay. Victor doesn't play around, damn it."

Kent said, "So what do we do?"

Ignoring the question, Jennifer continued, "I told you it was a bad idea to take you over there, but you wouldn't listen."

"I'll go over there," said Kent. "I'll straighten this thing out."

"Hell no. You can't go over there. The cops might be watching his place."

"How do you know?"

"I don't know for sure," said Jennifer. "But they could be."

Kent walked aimlessly around his room, his mind in a fog, anxiety setting in. He hadn't been able to sleep much, if any, in the passing days because the drugs prevented him from having a restful night's sleep. With that and the news of Felipe's assault, intensified paranoia stirred in his mind. He walked to his bedroom window, pulled the curtain, and looked nervously up and down his street. Parked alongside the curb were his truck and Jennifer's car. Thankfully, his mom was at work.

"This isn't good," said Kent. "This isn't good at all. I need to talk to Victor."

"No!" said Jennifer. "You can't. If you intervene, he's likely to do the same to you."

"No, he won't. He likes me."

"You only *think* he likes you. He's not one to mess with. This is what I've been trying to tell you. He's a dangerous man, Kent."

"I'm going over there," said Kent defiantly. He attempted to walk out of the room, but Jennifer grabbed him by the arm, stopping him. He snapped his arm from her grip and turned to her with an icy stare.

She said, "If you go over there, so help me God, I will leave you, Kent Weber. Stay away from Victor's house. I mean it!"

"Are you serious?"

"Try me," she answered. "I'm not playing around. I'm *dead serious.*"

Jennifer's threatening tone prompted Kent to recollect his rational thinking. He wanted to go to Victor's house, but he knew Jennifer was right. Not long after, he discarded the idea altogether. Going over there wouldn't fix the situation. The damage had been done. Felipe was in the hospital and there was nothing he could do about it.

"Then what should we do?" he asked out of desperation.

"We do nothing," said Jennifer. She paused. She grabbed her boyfriend's hand and then said something that Kent wasn't expecting her to say. "Don't you think maybe it's time we slowed down, you know, with the drugs? How much longer do you think our bodies can handle this abuse? We've been going hard, non-stop, for the last couple of months. Baby, you're leaving for Spalding tomorrow. Don't you think it's time to put all your focus there?"

This was the first time Kent had heard his girlfriend speak in such a way. He had indeed lost his focus, his vision, and also he had lost his passion for the game of basketball. There was a time, Kent remembered, when nothing else mattered. There was a time when he loved the competiveness, the self-discipline that the game instilled in him, and the camaraderie he'd had with his teammates. In reality, he'd lost sight of all that, of all the things he'd ever loved or ever known. It had all vanished, without him even realizing it.

"I just want to play basketball," said Kent. "That's all I've ever wanted to do." He pulled Jennifer closer.

"Then go play basketball, baby. Be the superstar that I know you can be. You can do it. I know you can."

"Thanks for believing in me," he said. "At least someone does."

*

When Kent opened his eyes, he flinched at the bright lights above. As he regained his focus, he looked down and, in his left arm, he noticed an IV with a hose that led up to a drip bag. A heart monitor beeped on the other side of the bed he was lying in. He looked around the room and realized it was a hospital room, and then remembered collapsing in the middle of the season opening game. Two familiar faces came to his bedside.

"Hey, kiddo," said the person who Kent recognized as his father.

"Hi, sweetheart," said Kent's mother.

Kent knew he didn't feel right, physically. His head throbbed and his chest ached.

There was a knock on the door and in walked the doctor who Kent now saw for the first time. He was a tall, slender man, with wavy blonde hair, wearing the traditional white doctor's coat, cradling a clipboard in his arm.

"How we doing?" he asked, looking down and flipping a few of the pages on his clipboard. He walked to the other side of Kent's bed. "Kent, I'm Dr. Andrews."

Wasting little time, Kent asked, "When can I get out of here?"

"Hopefully soon," said the doctor. "First, I need to go over a few things with you and your folks."

"Is everything okay, doc?" asked Kent's dad.

"Not as okay as it should be," he said. He looked to the clipboard. "The tests we ran confirmed your son had a heart attack, with a substantial amount of tissue damage. Also, Kent has severe erosion of the sinus and nasal cavity."

"I don't understand," said Kent's mom with confusion and worry on her face.

The doctor flipped the page back and put the clipboard under his arm. "I'm going to be straight with you, Mr. and Mrs. Weber. With the amount of heart damage Kent has, I'm afraid he won't be able to play basketball ever again. It'd be too risky."

"How much damage," Kent's dad asked.

"Well," the doctor began, "your son has the heart of a seventy-year-old man, instead of an eighteen-year-old boy."

Kent's dad stood from his chair. "Are you sure, doc? Is it that bad?"

"I'm afraid so."

"But how?" said Kent's mom. "Kent is the healthiest person I know. How can this be, at such a young age?"

Dr. Andrews scratched an itch at his temple and, again, flipped the pages on his clipboard until stopping on the fourth page.

"We also conducted a toxicology report and found something else. Kent had large amounts of methamphetamine in his system. We're almost certain the drug caused Kent's heart attack. We've been seeing many cases similar to Kent's, especially in younger people. I'm truly sorry, Mr. and Mrs. Weber. I truly am." The doctor looked down to Kent. "You should consider yourself lucky. Most people that come here in your condition don't recover as well as you have."

Kent's dad dropped his head, appearing overcome with shame. His mom idled back to her chair, sat down, and cried. Neither parent said anything to Kent.

The doctor then said, "I'll give you folks some time to be alone." His mouth curled upward into a tiny, sympathetic smile, and he walked out of the room.

Kent lay there in his hospital bed, painfully absorbing his father's disappointment and listening to his mother's relentless sobbing. He couldn't take it anymore. He wanted to run away. He wanted to go far, far away, but was unable. Off to his right, however, was a window and he turned his focus there, looking out into the crazy world. His room was on the ground floor and the only view was a crowded parking lot. It didn't matter to Kent; he wasn't looking at anything in particular, nor did he want to. Instead, his mind became consumed by the thoughts of his basketball career ending prematurely. *It wasn't supposed to be like this*, he thought. *This wasn't supposed to happen*. But sadly, it was happening.

As hard as he tried, Kent couldn't block out his mother's crying. He knew that he had let his parents down in a major way. At the beginning of his parents' divorce, Kent had accused them of being unsupportive, of bailing on his dreams. But now he knew that wasn't the case. He had been nothing more than selfish and stubborn, and it took something like this life-threatening incident to help him see the truth. It was all much clearer now. He turned back to his parents.

"Mom...Dad," he said in a voice filled with weakness and fear. "I think I might need...rehab. I think I might need help."

Wiping away her tears, his mother rose from her chair, and walked back to his bedside. Bending over to hug her son, she said nothing at all and, instead, cried a little harder. Kent's father walked over to join them. He looked down to his son. "Whatever you need, Kent," he said, fighting back his own tears. "As long as there's a breath in my body, I'll support you in any way I can. Your mother too. We'll always be here for you, son. No matter what. That's what parents are for."

"And your life isn't over. Not by a long shot," said Kent's mom through her tears. You can still continue with college and get your degree. You can be an elementary school teacher, like we had talked about."

"I know," said Kent. "I'll finish school. I promise. I just wish I had listened to you both, before all this got out of hand."

As Kent spoke, a few gentle knocks came from the door. Walking in was someone he hadn't seen or spoke to since he had left for college.

"Hey. It's me," said Jennifer softly.

"Hey, Jennifer," said Kent with an elated tone.

Jennifer walked to the bedside opposite of Kent's parents.

"Hello," she said.

Both parents nodded respectfully and said hello back.

Kent's mother said, "I think your father and I will leave you two alone for a bit—give you time to catch up."

"Thanks," said Kent. His mother gave him a kiss on the forehead and then headed toward the door. Kent's father soon followed.

"I got here as soon as could," said Jennifer. "I went to your game to surprise you."

"You were at my game?" asked Kent.

"Yeah. I didn't want to miss my baby's college debut."

Kent then explained to Jennifer of his heart attack, the reason he had collapsed in the middle of the game.

"The doctor said I can never play basketball again."

Jennifer said, "I'm so sorry, baby. I feel like this is all my fault. If I hadn't kept turning you on to that crap, or gotten you involved with Victor, then you wouldn't be lying here right now."

Kent then asked, "Did you ever find out what happened to Felipe?"

She said, "Felipe made it, Kent. I heard he's doing much better now."

"That's good," said Kent. "I didn't want him to die. I don't know that I could've lived with myself if he had."

"Me too," said Jennifer.

There were a few moments of silence.

Then Kent said, "I'm sorry I never returned your calls." He told her of a new drug connection that he had made on campus, of how his addiction had consumed him, keeping him away from friends and family.

"It's okay," said Jennifer. "I thought maybe you were really busy with school work and basketball practice."

"I can't do this anymore," he said. And all at once, he started to cry. He held nothing back, letting it all go. All the pent up aggression, all the debilitating pain, it all came pouring out of the tired, young man.

"I can get you into the treatment center that I go to," said Jennifer "They're a really great group of people. I'm positive that you'll like them."

"You would do that for me?" asked Kent, wiping his tears.

"Of course," said Jennifer.

"I'm ready for a change. I'm ready for all of this to be over."

Jennifer bent over to hug her boyfriend. "I believe in you. I know you can do it."

"Thanks for believing in me," said Kent. He squeezed Jennifer a little tighter.

"I've never stopped," she said.

After rehab, Kent returned to Spalding University where he obtained his degree in Elementary Education and became the schoolteacher that he had promised his mother he would become.

One afternoon while sitting at his desk, Kent observed his second grade class as they took their reading exam, and he reflected on those dark days of meth addiction. It was something he thought about often. And though he never admitted it, the drug was something that he still, from time to time, craved. But those grim feelings didn't last. All he had to do was look out in front of him and see those young, eager minds at work and think of how truly lucky a man he really was.

~~~

Best for the Family

Rachel pulled a photograph from her coat pocket and stared at the two people posing in it. Both were of a different time and place. Her eyes, solemn and downhearted, gazed at her six-year-old self, who stood next to her father. They both smiled graciously. Her yellow Easter dress reflected brightly in the sunshine and his sand-colored hair appeared wind-blown. Back then, she was daddy's little girl.

Life had seemed wonderful in those days, Rachel thought, still looking at the photograph. She reflected on the naivety that had once protected her youthful innocence. To be unaware of all that was heartless and cruel in the world was something that she considered sacred, especially now. But those days were long behind her. No more make-believe tea parties, no more Barbie fashion shows, no more being a child. All of it had vanished, but that's what she had wanted. To be an adult was all she ever had wanted.

Against her father's will, she had left Indiana three years before to venture west to pursue her big dream of becoming a world famous tattoo artist. At eighteen, she was of legal age, but that didn't stop Philip Sterling from trying to protect his little girl.

"You're making a big mistake, Rachel," he had said on the evening that she was to leave. "This is crazy. Nonsense, really. Tell her, Judy." Philip sought support from Rachel's mother. She however, turned away, ignoring the comment, not wanting to deal with either party.

"Why are you so against me doing this?" said Rachel, standing across the room with her hands on her hips. "All I've ever wanted to be was an artist. You know that."

All afternoon this bantering of strong wills had filled the Sterling home. Father and daughter went back and forth, each trying to convince the other of their noble intentions.

With patience exhausted, Philip pulled in a deep breath and said, "Sweetheart, I have nothing against you becoming an artist. I think it's a wonderful thing. But it's a bad idea for you to move so far away. That's all I'm saying."

"I'll be fine, Daddy. I have a job and a place to live when I get out there. I told you that. I wish you'd stop worrying so much."

Philip had heard enough. After everything he had done for his daughter, he couldn't believe she would defy him in this way.

"Okay," he said. "You win. You want to leave. You want to abandon your mother and me. Then go ahead. But when you get out there and you run out of money, or worse, don't come crawling back." Philip walked out of the kitchen and went out the side door to the garage, slamming the door behind him.

Mixed with sadness and anger, Rachel picked up her bags, kissed her mother good-bye, and walked out the front door. It was the last time she'd had any contact with her father.

While thinking back to that incident, Rachel ran a soft finger over her father's image in the photograph, and again wondered how everything had gone wrong. It was a long bus ride to the Indianapolis Heart Center, so she would have plenty of time to reflect.

While lost in yesteryear, Rachel heard a familiar voice beside her, one she had listened to for many miles. To her, it was a voice of age and wisdom. She snapped from her daydream.

"You've been admiring that picture for some time now," said the woman sitting in the bus seat next to Rachel. "You gonna let me see it?"

"Oh. Sorry," said Rachel. She held the picture out in front, giving the woman a better view.

"Now, look at that," said the woman. "That's a fine picture indeed. You best hang on to that forever. Family photos are a wonderful thing."

"I hope he's okay, Esther," said Rachel. "I don't think I could forgive myself if something happens to him." She observed the photograph once more, and then slid it back into her coat pocket.

The woman named Esther wore a brown dress covered with white polka dots. Across her lap was a small, burgundy handbag, of which she firmly held the handles. She released the bag and placed her dark, wrinkled hand on Rachel's knee.

"He'll be fine, child," she said. "You wait and see."

Rachel placed her young, pale hand on the elderly woman's. "I hope you're right."

Riding across the country, the old black woman with silver hair had become fast friends with the younger woman. She had listened and consoled Rachel. Though, up to this point, she had done more listening.

Rachel, with hair dyed black, and piercings in her ears, nose, and lip, had engaged in conversations of various sorts with her new friend. Mostly, however, she talked of her ailing father and their falling out.

"If he hadn't been so stubborn," said Rachel, "then none of this would've happened.

Esther grinned. To her, there was little doubt Rachel had acquired some of her father's stubbornness. It was obvious that Rachel was an eccentric, free-spirited young soul who didn't fashion to authority, which Esther admired.

"Sometimes a father has a hard time letting go of his little girl," said Esther. "Fear is what it was. He was afraid that if you moved away he wouldn't be able to take care of you, or protect you. He was scared of your adult independence."

Rachel said, "But that's just it. I don't need anyone to take care of me or protect me."

Esther thought the comment over, and then turned a little in her bus seat. "Child, you mind if I tell you a story?"

"Of course not," said Rachel.

Esther said, "I want to tell you about a couple little girls that I once knew and the relationship they had with their father. I think it may do you some good."

"Okay. Sure," said Rachel.

Esther spoke of a time about sixty years prior, when she was a child herself, around the age of ten. It was right after her mother's death, right after they had found her body in a shallow creek bed. In the beginning, no one really knew what had happened to her mother. Esther explained to Rachel that there was no *real* investigation because her mother was a black woman.

"That's terrible," said Rachel."

"Such were the times, child. Such were the times."

"Hardly seems right, though," said Rachel.

"A lot wasn't right in those days."

Esther explained how traumatic it had been to lose her mother, and not only for her, but for her older sister, Francine. It had also affected her father, Cole Higgins, who had changed from a loving and nurturing man to a calloused and cold-hearted monster. He especially showed no empathy for thirteen-year-old Francine.

"Where do you think you two are going?" he said one morning to his daughters who were heading toward the front door.

Both girls stopped. Francine shut her eyes and Esther noticed her sister's body tense. With school books in hand, the sisters reluctantly spun around to face their father.

"Why, Papa, we're going to school," said Francine, disguising her fear with the elated tone she often used. "Just like we do every morning."

"Don't sass me, girl," said Cole Higgins. "You ain't going nowhere until you get the firewood in and my breakfast fixed."

"But, Papa," Francine began, "I'll be late for school. And I've already bathed and got my good dress on."

"I don't give no mind about a damn dress. You do as you're told and get that wood in, ya hear?" Francine, saying nothing more, walked over to her mother's old sewing machine table to lay down her schoolbooks. Cole then said, "Make sure you fill that kindling box all the way up, too."

"Yes, Papa," she said.

"And don't cross-stack it, either."

"I won't, Papa."

"I'll help you," said Esther to her sister, running over to place her books on the sewing machine table.

"No, you won't," said Cole. "You get on to school."

"But, Papa, I can—"

"No buts. Get on to school before I strap ya good."

"Yes, Papa," said Esther. She grabbed her books and before walking out the door took one more look at Francine.

"I'll be fine, Esther," she said. "Soon as I get the kindling box filled and Papa's breakfast cooked, I'll be along."

Young Esther gave a subtle nod and walked out the front door. She knew Francine wouldn't make it to school that day, as she hadn't made it to school the two previous days either.

When Esther returned that afternoon, she saw a car parked out front, the same car she had seen for the last three days, the same car that belonged to her father's friend, Albert Buckley. Inside, she saw Francine's books still sitting on her momma's sewing machine table and her father slumped in his broken down chair. On her way to the kitchen, Esther also noticed the kindling box was still empty.

"Where's Francine?" she said.

"She's helping Albert in the back bedroom," said Cole Higgins. His eyes didn't move from the television set. A half-empty pint bottle of gin sat on the table beside his chair.

"Helping Albert?" she asked while rummaging through the cookie jar in search of a maple bar.

"She's helping him find a book, or something." He shifted almost nervously in his chair. "Don't ask so many damn questions, Esther."

"Can I go help?"

He swung his attention hard toward his youngest daughter. "No. You wait right there."

"Okay, Papa."

Esther plopped in a chair at the dinner table and began eating her maple bar. She waited for her older sister to come out of the back bedroom with her father's friend. Cole sat in his chair, laughing to himself, watching *I Love Lucy* on the small, fuzzed television screen, often reaching for the bottle at his side, swigging its contents.

Finally, two maple bars later, Esther watched as Albert Buckley emerged into the living room. He was a thin black man who wore baggy denim jeans and a dirty white t-shirt. He was much younger than her father was, Esther knew, but a lot older than either Francine or herself.

Albert walked out, tucking his shirt into the front of his pants. Esther also noticed that he had no book in his hand.

"Did you find your book?" asked Esther.

"What's that?" said Albert.

"Be quiet, Esther," her father interrupted. He lurched up from his chair and to his feet.

In an audible whisper, Albert said, "You mind if I come back tomorrow, Cole?" Esther watched the man hand her father a few crumpled dollar bills.

Ester's father hesitated, and then said, "Yeah, sure. Tomorrow evening, though." He took the money and stuffed it in his front pants pocket. He sank again into his chair and reached for the bottle of gin.

Albert smiled a toothy, yellow grin. "Will do, Cole, will do." The man lifted his hat and jacket off the coat rack, smiled at Esther, and headed out the front door.

Esther cringed. Even at the young age of ten, she knew evil, and she knew evil would return. It always had.

Esther ran to the back room that she shared with Francine, and saw her older sister sitting on the edge of the bed, staring down to the floor. She seemed oblivious to her little sister entering the room.

"Francine," Esther began. "You okay?" The little girl waited for an answer. With no response, Esther jumped up into the air and flopped down next to her sister on the edge of the bed, causing both to bounce. Without an answer still and desperate for attention, she said, "Hello?"

"Go away," said Francine. She shifted on the bed's edge, turning her back to Esther.

"Don't be that way, Francine. You want to go outside and play?" She continued to bounce on the bed.

"Just go away," said Francine. "And stop doing that."

"Come on. We can go out to the apple tree and collect the rotten ones off the ground and throw them at Simon and Eddie when they go riding by—like we always do."

"I don't want to. I just want to be by myself."

"What were you guys doing in here?" asked Esther.

"Just doing what Papa wants me to do."

"Oh," said Esther, but still not understanding. She stopped bouncing, and sat quietly. She picked a tiny scab on her knee until a droplet of blood welled up. She dabbed her finger in it.

"You're disgusting," said Francine.

"Here, have some," said Esther, acting as though she might rub her bloody fingertip on her sister.

Francine said, "Don't even try it." She grabbed Esther's wrist, and both girls twisted and tugged at one another until they ended up on the floor, rolling around.

The next day, on the way home from school, Esther again brought up the topic of Albert Buckley.

"Are you ever going to tell me what you guys do back there in our bedroom?"

"You're too young to understand," said Francine.

"I asked Papa, but he wouldn't tell me."

"Don't worry about it," said Francine, raising her voice. "You wouldn't understand. Besides, Papa says it's best for the family."

"What's best for the family?"

"You ask too many questions."

"Yeah, so what," said Esther. And then she said something that Francine wasn't expecting. "I did see what he was doing to you—one time. I mean...I sort of did."

Francine stopped abruptly on the sidewalk. She clutched her little sister by the arm, causing her to halt also. She glared at Esther.

"Just what do you mean?"

"Let go, Francine. You're hurting me." The little girl yanked her arm, finally freeing it from her sister's grip.

"What did you see, Esther?"

Where her sister had squeezed her arm, Esther rubbed it and said, "The other day when Papa fell asleep in his chair, like he always does, I tiptoed to the back bedroom, and peeked through the crack of the door. That's all."

"What else?" Francine demanded.

"Not much," said Esther. "I looked in and Albert was on top of you, under the covers, moving around. But I wasn't sure what he was doing. Then I hurried back to the front room before Papa saw me. I knew he would strap me good if he caught me."

Francine said, "I ought to strap you myself. Don't ever go sneaking around like that again. You hear me! What I do in the bedroom is none of your business." She stormed off, leaving Esther standing alone on the sidewalk.

Esther hurried to catch her big sister, running up alongside her. "I'm sorry, Francine. I didn't mean anything by it. I didn't know I was doing anything bad."

Francine then finally said, "Just don't ever do it again."

"I won't," said Esther.

The sisters continued their walk home when a voice yelled out.

"Hey there, young ladies. How you two doing today?"

Esther waved and said, "Hi, Carl," and ran over to the man wearing the deputy sheriff's uniform. Francine hesitantly followed. "You find anything out about my momma, yet?" she asked.

"I'm sorry, sweetheart," said Carl. "Sheriff Baker hasn't released any information."

Esther dropped her head. "Hopefully he will soon."

"I hope so too," said the Deputy Sheriff. He then said, "How's school going?"

"Good," said Esther. "I'm making good marks all the way across."

"That's great. How about you, Francine?"

Francine didn't answer. She was still thinking about what Esther had told her, about what she had seen in the bedroom. A sickness stirred within the pit of her stomach, like the one that came back each time Albert Buckley made his visits.

Carl asked, "Francine, you okay?"

Her face lacked any emotion. "School's going great. Couldn't be better. Esther, we should be going. Papa will start worrying if we don't get home soon. See you later, Carl," she said all in one breath and started back toward the sidewalk. "Come on, Esther." She clutched her sister by the arm.

Esther shrugged. "See you later, Carl."

"Would you like me to walk you the rest of the way home?"

"No, that's okay," said Francine. "We can manage. Come on, Esther. Let's go."

"Okay then, see you later," said the Deputy Sheriff. "Tell your papa I said hello and that I'll be by to visit soon."

"Okay, I will," yelled Esther, looking back over her shoulder as her sister dragged her away.

Walking home, Esther thought more about her sister's situation. She still didn't know what was happening in the bedroom between her and Albert, but whatever was going on was causing Francine heartache and grief, something she didn't like to see coming from the one she loved and cared for more than anything in the entire world.

Even though she had a good idea of what the answer would be, Esther asked, "You like going back there in the bedroom with Albert?"

"No," said Francine. "He's dirty and his breath smells bad."

"Then, don't go back there. Tell Papa you don't like it."

"I can't," said Francine. "I tried once, but he got mad and wouldn't listen."

"Maybe you could tell someone else."

"Like who?"

"Maybe Aunt Vera? Or...Carl? You could tell your teacher, Mrs. Callahan."

"Aunt Vera lives too far away and Carl probably wouldn't listen. Besides, he and Papa are good friends. And Mrs. Callahan...I don't know. Seems like a lot of trouble. I'm better off doing what Papa tells me."

"We have to try *something*, Francine."

"Don't worry about it, Esther. You're too young to worry about things like this."

"But—"

"I said don't worry about it." Francine spoke in an agitated whisper as she and Esther approached the front door of their home. "Everything will be fine. Papa isn't working and I have to do what's best for the family."

That evening, Esther sat on the sofa—enforced by her father—while Francine waited in her bedroom.

"Why can't I go back there with Francine, Papa?" she asked, not looking at her father. She sat admiring a doll made from old rags which had been stuffed and sewn with newspaper. It was one her mother had made for her a few years back. She didn't play with dolls anymore, not like when she was younger, but she did admire this doll. She
fiddled with the little glued-on buttons that ran down the front. She said, "Why is it sometimes I can go back there and sometimes I can't?"

Cole Higgins sat in his broken down chair, watching television, drinking his gin.

"Not now, Esther," he said, trying to keep his concentration on the T.V. screen. "You can go back there later when—" A knock on the door interrupted his words. "Come in," he said. In through the door walked Albert Buckley.

"Howdy, Cole," he said, smiling with his yellow-stained teeth.

"In the back."

Albert headed to the back backroom, and when he passed Esther he said, "Well, ain't you growing up to be just as pretty as your big sister." He shook his head, appearing overjoyed with the pleasurable fantasies in his head.

"Just do what you got to do and hurry the hell up," said Cole.

"Yeah. Sure thing," said Albert. Again, he glanced to Esther before disappearing to the back bedroom. She shot him a cold stare that could have iced over a lake of fire.

When Albert was out of sight, Esther said, "I don't like him, Papa. I don't like him going back there. Why do you let him? He does bad things to Francine." She spoke to her father in a way she never had before, bold and forthright.

"Shut your damn mouth, Esther," he said. "It ain't no concern of yours."

Normally, Esther listened to her father. She had never crossed him, never gone against him. But this time was different. She had committed and there was no stopping now.

"No, Papa," she said. "You shut *your* mouth! My sister is back there with Albert. I don't know what he's doing, but I know Francine doesn't like it." Then fear replaced her anger. She tried to swallow, but her mouth was too dry. Clutching her doll, she scooted back into the cushion of the sofa, trying to hide, trying to escape what she knew was coming.

Cole Higgins set his gin bottle on the table beside him, wiped the alcohol that rolled down his chin, and started to stand. He gripped one arm of the chair and then the other, pushing himself up slowly to his unsteady legs. He wobbled a little and faced Esther.

"Well, look what we have here," he slurred. His lips were moist and shiny and his eyes were bloodshot. Esther thought he appeared skinny and old, well past his true age of forty-five. "Looks like little Esther has some gumption about her after all—just like her papa." The comment came in a swelling, prideful sort of way, which shocked and confused the little girl. Cole advanced toward Esther.

"Now, don't get me wrong," he started again. He rolled his eyes up and to the right, not looking at Esther. "Your momma..." He cleared his throat. "Your momma, may God rest her whorin' soul, had some gall, too. She wouldn't take no guff from nobody. Not even me." He shifted his eyes back down to Esther. "But we all see where that got her."

"Papa, sit down. You're drunk," said Esther. She saw the face of evil coming in her direction. She stood, attempting a getaway, but Cole was there, blocking her path.

Grabbing Esther by the arm, he yanked and flung her to the floor where she skinned her knee and sprained her wrist. The rag doll flew across the room, sliding on the floor until stopping underneath the supper table.

Throughout the years, Esther had endured her share of knocks and bruises by fighting with her older sister. She was used to a pummel or two, so the sprained wrist and skinned knee didn't hurt much. Even so, like the doll, she too sought refuge under the table.

"Get out of there, girl," said Cole in a non-threatening voice, a voice that was too calm to trust. "Get out here and take what you got comin' to ya."

From under the table, Esther watched as her father's boots scooted across the floor in her direction. She retreated backward until stopping where the wall met the table. She squeezed her doll, hugging it for safety and assurance.

As Cole slung a chair out of his way, a yell came from the back room. Then, a scream from Francine. He stopped at the sound of thudding footsteps. Albert Buckley entered the living room. His pants were on, but not his shirt. In one hand, he held a shoe, and with the other, he cupped his genitals.

"Damn that girl," he said. "She kneed me real good, Cole!"

"I don't care," said Cole. "Give me my money."

Albert started for the door. "I ain't giving you nothing."

Cole tried to pursue, but Albert was too fast and Cole was too drunk. The front door slammed and Albert was gone.

"Fuck!" he said.

Infuriated, Cole headed toward the back bedroom. Although keeping her distance, Esther crawled from under the supper table and followed.

Cole charged into the room as Francine was putting the last of her clothes on. Her nose trickled blood.

"What the hell's wrong with you?" said Cole. "Why'd you run that poor boy off like that?"

Francine said, "It's because I'm through with this, Papa. I'm done. I'm not doing it anymore!"

"Like hell you ain't," said Cole and started at Francine.

Francine tried running past her father. With one arm, he scooped her up around her stomach, and slammed her back onto the bed. He came at her once again.

"You and your sister want to go against me...well, you both will learn the hard way—just like your momma did." When he got to the side of the bed that Francine was on, he squeezed his hands around her neck.

Esther screamed. With unwavering courage, she leaped to the top of the mattress and jumped on the back of Cole Higgins.

"Get off her!" said Esther. From behind, she sank her fingers deep into her father's eyes, while screaming for his mercy. Sharp claws dug deeper and deeper.

In an instant, Cole released his grip from Francine's throat and pried the knife-like nails from his eyes. He threw Esther on the bed, beside her gasping, choking sister.

Cole blinked until regaining his vision and again came at his daughters.

He said, looking at Francine, "You don't want to do this anymore? Well, you don't have to 'cause I'm gonna break both of your damn necks and throw you in the creek—like I did your momma." The girls screamed. About that time, they watched as their father went wide-eyed. He grasped and tugged at the object around his neck, the object cutting off his air supply. Deputy Sheriff Carl Mosley held firm to the nightstick.

"Get out of here, you two!" said Carl as he wrestled Cole Higgins to the floor.

The girls fled the bedroom, making their way outside.

Standing on the front lawn, Esther heard the loud commotion continue inside the house as Deputy Sheriff Carl tried to subdue her drunken father. In a few passing moments, the banging and shuffling stopped. With worry and fear, the sisters waited until the front door opened and both watched as Carl Mosley escorted, in handcuffs, their father to the patrol car parked alongside the curb.

"It's okay, girls," said Cole Higgins, his face bloodied and battered. "I'll be home soon. Don't worry." He tried slowing his pace, but Deputy Sheriff Carl gave a mighty shove.

Eerily chilled, Rachel listened as Esther told the story from long ago.

"So what happened to your father?" asked Rachel.

"He died in prison, child. He admitted to the authorities that he was the one who killed my momma. Never saw him again after that night."

"Oh," said Rachel, shocked. "And Albert?"

"They found his body in a shallow grave just outside of town about a month after that night." She then said, "Sometimes, I sit and think about how me and Francine almost died that night. If Carl Mosley hadn't come to visit my father, you might not be talking to me right now. After Francine and I went to stay with our Aunt Vera, I wrote to him many times to thank him. He was a godsend for sure."

Rachel's mind went back to her own father. She wanted to tell him she was sorry. She wanted to tell him how much she had missed him. But most of all, she wanted to tell him how much she loved him. She only hoped it wasn't too late.

Not long after, the bus rolled to its stop at the Indianapolis bus station. Esther, Rachel, and about a dozen other people filed onto the concrete curb. They waited as the driver unloaded their bags from the storage compartments.

"Is this where we say our good-byes?" said Rachel. She grabbed the handle of her suitcase. "I'm going to miss you, Esther."

Esther also clutched the handle of her roll-behind suitcase. "Lord sakes, child. This isn't good-bye. This is *until we meet again*." With their free arms, each woman wrapped the other with an affectionate embrace, as any two long-time friends would have done.

"I'm so glad I met you," said Rachel.

"Me too," said Esther. "And remember, you and your father will be just fine. When you get to the hospital, you tell him so. And tell him how much you love him."

"I will," said Rachel. "Tell Francine I said hello, too."

"No need of that," said Esther. "You can tell her yourself."

Rachel spun to see an elderly woman, looking much like Esther, hobble up to where they stood. Esther let loose of her suitcase handle to hug her older sister.

"It's so good to see you," said Francine to her younger sister. "How was the ride? Terrible I'm sure."

"It was nice, actually," said Esther. She smiled at Rachel. "I enjoyed it very much."

"We better get going," said Francine. "I've big plans for us."

"Francine," Esther began. "I want you to meet this sweet, young woman who I had the pleasure of talking with on the ride over. This is Rachel."

She was unsure of how to respond to the strange looking girl who had jewelry sticking out of her face. But when Rachel smiled and stuck out her hand, Francine did the same.

"It's nice to meet you," said Rachel. "Esther has told me a lot about you."

"I'm not surprised at all," said Francine, poking fun at her sister. "She's always been one for talking."

After another quick hug and good-bye between Esther and Rachel, the sisters departed and Rachel found her mom who had been waiting in the bus depot lobby.

"How's Dad doing?" asked Rachel.

"He's stable for now," said her mom. "He could go either way."

"But he has a chance, right?"

"The doctors are saying 50/50. The heart attack did a lot of damage, sweetheart. We can only hope and pray from here on out."

When Rachel and her mother made it to the hospital and walked into her father's recovery room, her heart sank. Unconscious, Philip Sterling laid helpless, wires and hoses running to and from his body. Rachel walked to his bedside, seeing him for the first time in three years.

At first, she said nothing. Instead, she prayed silently and thought of the day that they'd had their falling out, which made her cry. She thought of her friend Esther and her story. This recollection only reinforced her belief in the pettiness of her and her father's original disagreement.

Why did I have to be so stubborn? she thought.

Looking down to her father, she realized she might not get the chance to apologize. She placed her head beside her father's head and cried onto his pillow. She whispered into his ear.

"I'm so sorry, Daddy, for the way I acted. You were right. I shouldn't have gone prancing clear across the country chasing some crazy dream. I know you were just scared of losing me—your little girl. But I'll always be your little girl. No matter what. I love you, Daddy."

Rachel stood and pulled the picture of her and her father from her coat pocket. She placed the photograph on the pillow and leaned over to kiss his forehead. As she went to take a seat in the empty chair beside her mother, she heard a whimper and then a moan behind her. With a smile stretching across her face, she watched as Philip Sterling's eyelids gradually peeled apart.

"Hi...Daddy," said Rachel, fighting back more tears.

With his dry, raspy voice, Philip said to his daughter, "Hey, sweetheart." The corner of his mouth curved upward, into a tiny smile. "I'm glad you're here."

Standing at her father's side, with tears rolling down her face and onto the bed sheet, Rachel said, "I'm glad to be here, Daddy. I've missed you, and I'm sorry for everything."

Philip, weak and in pain, lifted his hand and rested it on his daughter's.

"I've missed you too, baby girl."

Father and daughter looked into each other's eyes and decided, with unspoken words, to forget the enduring heartache that each had caused the other. Esther was right: everything would truly be fine.

~~~

Secret Lovers

The truck's headlights reflected off the cottony snowflakes that floated down from the night sky. The road was isolated and hardly a car passed in the opposite direction. Charity Richards sat in the passenger seat casually stroking her knuckle where her wedding ring had been for the last five years. By instinct, she felt again in her front pants pocket to make sure the ring was still there. In her mind, she kept telling herself that her marriage was over, that she was doing no wrong.

Scott Weston drove his truck through tight curves as if he were trying to get a rise from his passenger. When the truck came into a straightaway, he glanced to Charity, waiting for her reaction.

"She handles great, doesn't she?" he said.

"This snow is really falling," said Charity. "Maybe you should slow down."

Scott eased his foot from the accelerator, bringing the truck down to a safer speed.

"That better?"

"Yes, thank you."

"Are you okay?" he said, noticing her uneasiness.

Again, Charity rubbed her finger. "A little nervous—that's all."

"No reason to be nervous," Scott said. He reached over and put his hand on her plump thigh. "Don't worry, everything is fine. Tonight is going to be great." He rubbed her leg. "I have a surprise planned for you."

Charity wasn't used to surprises.

"And what might that be?" she said.

"Can't tell you. It's a secret."

The strange but affectionate hand on her leg felt comforting. A long time had passed since anyone had shown her attention like this. There was a warm emotion stirring inside of her and it was a pleasant and inviting change. She was a young and lonely woman who needed love. Her husband, Dustin, although he did love his wife, had not expressed any feelings toward her in two years.

"Okay," she said in a vulnerable, childlike voice. "I guess I can wait."

"I know you're going to love it," said Scott.

She had been to the cabin before. She had come with Dustin to a party hosted by Scott and one of his girlfriends at the time. When they arrived, Scott flipped on the lights and the accommodations were quaint and calming, just as Charity had remembered them. A creek-stone fireplace burned and crackled from across the room. A bottle of wine and two glasses sat over on the dining room table.

Charity looked around and again tried to convince herself that this was acceptable behavior for a woman whose husband was no longer interested in her or their love life.

Scott threw his keys on the counter and turned to Charity, putting his hands on her waist, pulling her closer.

"You need to relax," he said. "You're so tense." He bent over to kiss her thin, pale lips, but she turned away, allowing him only a peck on her cheek.

When Scott let loose and stepped away she said, "I know. I'm trying, I really am. I do like you."

He walked to the dining room table, slipped out of his coat, and hung it on the back of one of the chairs. He opened the bottle of wine and she stared at him as he poured it into the glasses. He was a handsome man, and she had always thought so. He was taller than her husband and in much better shape although Dustin at one time had taken excellent care of himself. He worked out, watched his diet, but lost interest in his health regimen as the years passed, letting himself go—his looks, his waistline. Charity, on the other hand, had worked strenuously at looking attractive for her unnoticing husband. Finally, though, someone had noticed her. She was tired of feeling lonely, tired of feeling unloved.

With his back turned, Scott said, "I like you too. I only want this night to be great for the both of us." He faced her again and offered her one of the glasses of wine.

"Me too," she said.

Charity took off her coat and made her way over to the sofa. Scott walked to the fireplace and stoked the flames with a poker. He grabbed a small log from the stack on the hearth to throw in, and then sat next to Charity.

Her first glass of wine relaxed her mind and she began to enjoy the company of the man who appreciated her, who listened to what she had to say. She thought it felt nice and she was ready for a change in her life. She scooted closer to Scott.

"I'm glad I came," she said.

"I'm glad you came too," he said.

Charity sighed. Those words were soothing to hear. A long time had passed since she had experienced this kind of feeling, a feeling of being wanted and appreciated. Tonight she was feeling all that and so much more.

The thought of being caught never entered her mind, really. Her story was solid. She was having a girl's night out with her best friend, Erica, is what she had told Dustin. And if she had too much to drink, she would stay overnight. She had left her car at Erica's house also, where Scott had picked her up earlier. Erica was on board with the plan and knew to stick with the story if Dustin began asking questions.

"Sure, girl," Erica had said. "I've got you covered. Go have fun. You deserve it."

Sitting on the couch, drinking wine and cuddling, Charity and Scott laughed together and told their intimate feelings to each other.

"I've always thought you were sexy as hell," said Scott.

"You did not," said Charity, as the flames from the fireplace reflected brightly on her face, showing her huge smile.

"I swear," he said. "Didn't you ever see me checking you out?"

She had thought it once, but was sure that a gorgeous guy like Scott Weston would never be interested in a short, dumpy, married woman like her.

"Whatever," she said, feeling her face turn as red as the glowing coals in the fireplace.

Again, Scott leaned in to kiss her as he had at the front door. This time, she didn't turn away. The wine made her brave and her lips touched his. She embraced the man for the first time, the man who claimed to be her husband's friend.

A roaring passion engulfed Charity, and Scott sensed this from her willingness to dive further into the depths of infidelity, not holding back, pulling down all barricades. Their sexual intensity climbed, and he freed his mouth from hers long enough to pry the condom from the front pocket of his jeans. Moments later, in the heat of entangled passion, the secret lovers were on the floor where their shadows cascaded on the cabin wall, moving as one, moaning and writhing.

In the beginning of Charity's marriage, there were spontaneous moments—like the one she was experiencing now with Scott. One day, Dustin had ravished her, surprising her as she walked through the door—coming home from a hard day's work—by bending her over the kitchen table. The blowjob on the hiking trail was another spur of the moment sexual impulse. But their moments of intimacy
never progressed. It had become a chore or a duty to perform or satisfy the other one. For Charity, it was even troublesome to get Dustin in the mood. She tried the basic offerings: sexy lingerie at bedtime, porn, excessive petting in all the right spots, but nothing grabbed his attention. Before long, as many couples do, they had lost their way.

Scott stood and stepped into his pants while Charity remained on the floor. Her large, naked breasts twinkled with sweat as her chest rose and fell. She sighed and let out a carefree giggle.

"What's so funny?" said Scott as he tossed the condom and wrapper in the fireplace.

"Nothing." Her smile widened. "Everything is perfect."

"I'm glad you're enjoying yourself," said Scott, pulling his head through his sweater.

"I'm glad I came," she said. A few silent moments passed, and she said, "Aren't you?"

With his back turned, pouring a glass of wine, he said, "Yeah...sure."

Charity stood, slipped into her jeans, and then put on her bra and shirt.

"You don't sound as convincing as you did a few minutes ago," she said, settling on the end of the sofa.

Scott handed her another full glass of wine and sat beside her.

"Everything's fine. Promise. You still have your surprise coming, you know."

"I haven't forgotten," said Charity. She tipped her glass to drink and stared out of the corner of her eye at Scott.

"It's going to be great. I know you're going to love it," he said.

Charity licked the tartness of red wine from her lips. "I never would've guessed this in a million years."

"Guessed what?" he asked.

"*This*," she said. "Me cheating on Dustin. Us being together. I can't believe you were ever interested in me. I didn't think I was your type. You've always dated the skinny blondes."

Scott took a sip from his glass and checked his cell phone. "Would you relax? I think you're sexy. I told you I've always thought that."

"I know," said Charity. "It's nice to hear it said out loud from time to time. Dustin never tells me anymore."

"Dustin is a good guy," said Scott. "He's smart as hell and successful. You couldn't ask for much more."

"I know," Charity agreed. "But he is so wrapped up in his business that he's forgotten about *us*."

"You should be glad he's trying to make something of himself."

"I am, but he never—" She stopped. A scowl contorted her face. "Why are you suddenly defending him? That's a little ironic, don't you think?"

Scott guzzled more from his glass. "I don't think so. He's a good guy. I've always thought that of Dustin, you know that."

Surprised, Charity said nothing. Instead, she motioned for the wine bottle sitting on the floor at the end of the sofa. She stuck out her glass and Scott topped her off. He did the same to his glass. She drank again while trying to cope with the strange situation in which she had put herself. The wine was working. She felt her cheeks numbing and warming with each glass. She didn't usually drink much, but she liked the buzzy, tingly feeling in her head. It also helped lighten the mood.

She sensed the evening veering off course and changed the subject.

"Are you ever going to tell me about this *surprise*?" she asked.

Scott said, "Not much longer. I promise." Again, he put his hand on her leg.

Charity shifted in her seat. She put her hand on Scott's, stopping him from going further up her leg.

"What is it?" he said.

"Nothing."

"You can tell me."

She paused and then said, "There is something. Something I need to get off my chest."

Scott said nothing. His face fixed with intrigue.

Charity held Scott's hand a little tighter and said, "I'm leaving Dustin as soon as I get back. I'm packing my things and leaving."

"Are you sure that's what you want to do?" he said.

"It's falling apart. You've seen it. Our marriage has been in shambles for a long time. I'm not happy. He's not happy. It's time to move on."

"I guess you know what's best," said Scott with a hint of sarcasm. "But I still stand by what I said: Dustin is a good guy. I think if you gave him a chance. You know?"

Again, Charity gave a perplexed look. "Wow. You're really stuck on defending him."

"I'm not *stuck* on anything," said Scott. "I'm simply expressing my opinion of the man. That's all."

Charity sipped again from her glass and then said, "I thought you'd be happy about me leaving him."

"Why would I be happy about that?" He glanced again to his cell phone.

The evening again was going astray, and Charity put her hand on Scott's muscular leg and massaged. "I thought tonight would be the start of something special between you and me."

Where this was heading made Scott squirm in his seat. He didn't want to fall in love or break up a marriage, or even start an affair with his buddy's wife. This night was about having a good time, getting a piece of ass, and moving on, like all the other times. Besides, Charity knew he had had many girlfriends and fly by night flings in all the years she had known him. Why would she think *this* would be any different?

"Look," Scott started, "there is something we should probably get out of the way. I don't want to hurt your feelings but—"

"Knock knock," said a woman's voice.

Scott stood from the sofa, a giant grin on his face.

Barging in, a woman with blonde hair wearing black jeans, a grey winter coat, and white boots, stomped her feet, knocking off the excess snow.

"Well, it's about time you showed," said Scott with playful sarcasm.

"Hey, I made it, didn't I?" said the woman. Passing Scott, she walked to the warm fireplace.

Charity eyed the girl. She didn't know her. She didn't look familiar. She was about to introduce herself when the blonde spotted her on the sofa.

"Hey," she said casually. "I'm Nikki. You must be Charity."

"Hey," said Charity, and drank from her glass.

Nikki took off her coat, threw it on the floor, and went over to sit on the opposite end of the sofa.

"That wine looks good," she said. "Mind if I help myself?"

"Not at all," said Charity.

She picked up the bottle from the floor and drank freely, emptying the contents in a few massive gulps. She sat the bottle back on the floor and licked her lips.

"I haven't drunk wine in forever," said the girl named Nikki. "I forgot how much I liked it."

Scott walked over and sat in the middle of the couch, in the middle of the two women.

Charity looked at Scott and said, "So what's going on here?"

"I thought we could amp up the evening by throwing Miss Nikki into the mix." He turned to the blonde and said, "You're down, right?"

"I wouldn't be here if I wasn't," she said. And then, "You guys have any more wine?"

"In the fridge," Scott said.

She went to the refrigerator and Charity, in a calm whisper, said, "This was totally not the surprise I was expecting."

"But I thought you were into this sort of thing," said Scott.

"You mean *girls?*" she said. "Why would you think that?"

"Well...you know...you did make-out with that one chick."

Thinking, she had recalled the incident. It happened at a party she and Dustin had hosted at their house. And it had been a playful kiss with Erica, on a dare. Hardly a make-out session.

"That was us just goofing around and being silly," she said.

"So I take it you're not okay with this."

"No. Not really," she said.

"Are you sure? This could be a lot of fun."

Charity thought that maybe it would be fun. This would be something new, something different, that's for sure. At one time, she had even considered bringing in a third party to liven up her and Dustin's sex life, but it never got any further than a twinkling thought.

"Some other time," she said. "Maybe you should take me back to my car."

"You sure?" said Scott.

She nodded.

"Okay. Whatever you want."

Charity got out of Scott's truck and noticed the lights were off inside Erica's house, so she didn't bother knocking. It was 2 a.m. and she decided she was sober enough to drive home.

The snowing had stopped, but Charity still drove slower than usual. She took her time, contemplating the next move in her marriage. She had told Scott she was leaving Dustin. But was she really? She had said those words when thinking there was a real chance that she and he could start a relationship, a new life together.

Now, she was having second thoughts. Maybe she would try to make her marriage work with Dustin after all. It was true however, that she had lain with another man. Their marriage had been tainted and she was now feeling the extreme guilt caused by it. But she didn't have to mention it to Dustin, and with enough passing time, the guilt would subside and they could go on as if nothing had happened. She could never tell Dustin of this night. It would devastate him. This night would be better forgotten, forever.

Her car stopped in the driveway and she killed the engine. She pulled her wedding ring from her pocket and slipped it back onto her finger, and vowed silently to never take it off again. She loved Dustin, and that was the way it was going to be.

She tiptoed easily through the front door and shut it behind her quietly, as if she were a teenager all over again, sneaking in from a late night, well past curfew. But she was doing this only out of respect. Dustin could become irritable if awakened in the middle of the night. Her plan was to slip upstairs unnoticed, shower, and crawl into bed with her husband.

Instead of flipping the switch at the bottom of the stairway, Charity pulled her cellphone from her purse and lit the way. Gently she paced up each step, knowing where to place her foot to avoid the loud creakiness for which the old stairs were known. Arriving at the top, she heard the faint sound of music coming from down the hallway, from the direction of her and Dustin's bedroom. A light from the doorway cast a soft glow on the opposite wall. She put her phone back into her purse and walked toward her bedroom.

Maybe Dustin was up late working, she thought.

He sometimes would work into the early hours of the morning, answering emails from potential clients, or writing code for new website templates. Even though she had become annoyed by his work ethic, she had to agree with Scott: Dustin had worked hard to achieve every ounce of his success. She couldn't dispute that.

Arriving within a few feet of the bedroom door, she heard fitful moans and sighs mixed with the melody of R & B music. Turning the corner of the bedroom door, she saw two naked bodies having their way with one another. Straddling her husband was Erica, her friend, riding the man who for the last two years had hardly looked her way, the man who had lost interest in his marriage and his wife.

Unseen, Charity fought back her tears and slowly retreated into the hallway. Her breaths became staggered and difficult to manage. She headed back down the stairs in a fit, out the front door, and back into her car where her tires spun out in the gravel driveway. She sped wildly down the darkened country road, sobbing, not knowing her destination, her future, or the future of her marriage.

~~~

JEREMY PERRY is a short story writer who lives in southern Indiana. He creates tales that enchant imaginations, provoke thoughts and feelings, and give rushing jolts of engaging entertainment. In his spare time he enjoys watching classic films and television.

Printed in Great Britain
by Amazon.co.uk, Ltd.,
Marston Gate.